A Sneeze to Die For

Piney Woods, Volume 2

Teresa Trent

Published by Teresa Trent, 2024.

A SNEEZE TO DIE FOR

First edition. April 23, 2024.

Copyright © 2024 Teresa Trent.

ISBN: 979-8990262621

Written by Teresa Trent.

Chapter 1

Alan Shaw rang a small silver bell in a staccato pattern.

The bell, which usually rested on the check-in desk, was in his hand as he stood by a computer in the office center the hotel provided. He reached over and plugged a USB thumb drive into the side of one of the machines and attempted to turn the computer on. As he waited for it to boot up, he continued to hammer on the annoying little device. Nora managed to smile.

The Meow Meetup, a gathering of cat lovers, would be the first official convention at the Tunie Hotel since Nora had bought a partnership in the business. This man was most likely their first guest for the event. With full occupancy at the Tunie, this little get-together would help Nora and her partner, Marty Reynolds, to stay in the black. Even though she was nervous, having a convention in a forty-room hotel in East Texas was exciting.

Shaw, unimpressed with her dazzling smile, continued to ring the bell.

Nora moved into his line of sight. "Can I help you? I'd be glad to help you at the front desk." She gestured toward the check-in area. The short, pudgy man was more than a little perturbed and had shown it through his use of the tinny bell.

He followed her over, and then, leaning on the counter, wedged his worn black high tops between his cheap leatherette bags. "Glad to know you could work me into your busy schedule," he said, his voice crisp.

"I'm sorry for your inconvenience. How may I help you? Are you checking in for the Meow Meetup?"

"The Meow Meetup? Really?" The little man gave Nora a look, clearly disgusted with her and the cutesy name of the convention. "To be blunt, the last thing I'd like to do is check into this fleabag motel to cover a conference with an ill-chosen location, but needs must. Piney Woods, Texas? Who chooses a place like this? Did you know you can smell... livestock out there?"

Nora's chin rose at his insults. He was typical of someone from a large city who considered anything outside of his area inadequate. Next, he would start asking about bedbugs, and, as for the livestock smell, what did he expect? He was in Texas. She ignored his comment and attempted to put on her best hospitality face. "Welcome to Piney Woods. Let me look up your reservation."

"Shaw. Allen Shaw. Hopefully, your clerk didn't write my reservation on his tobacco chaw wrapper."

"I assure you, sir. We have a state-of-the-art check-in system that doesn't require chewing tobacco wrappers to document our reservations." Nora gave the little rat another smile and typed his name into the computer. She waited for the reservation confirmation to come up as she watched the spinning cursor, signifying the computer was busy.

Result not found.

The "state-of-the-art" system didn't seem to know he existed. Nora typed in the man's name again, hoping it would appear. Still, the results of her search came up with nothing. Alan Shaw was not registered at the hotel. Maybe it was on chewing tobacco paper somewhere?

"How do you spell Alan?" Nora asked.

The man harrumphed. "A-L-A-N. It's the standard spelling for the name. Any idiot knows that." Nora wanted to tell him she wasn't just any idiot. She was the lucky idiot who had to deal with him. She tried it one more time with alternate spellings. Still nothing. The hotel was booked solid for the Meow Meetup convention.

"When did you make your reservation?"

Alan let out an exasperated sigh, his full lips fluttering. "I don't know. My secretary made it for me last week sometime."

"I'm very sorry, Mr. Shaw, but it doesn't seem there is a reservation on record for you."

He scowled. "I should have known better staying at a podunk hotel like this. A national chain would have never screwed up a simple thing like a reservation." He turned his rounded head to the side and spoke to Nora as if she were a child. "Okie-dokie. Make me a reservation. I will be here for the extent of the cat conference, and I would like a room with a view of the street, not the back alley."

Nora checked her screen one more time to make sure there weren't any last-minute cancellations. Incredibly, the Tunie Hotel had 100 percent occupancy for the first time in years. Unfortunately, she would have to tell this angry man that he was not on the guest list. "Again, our apologies, but we don't have any vacancies right now."

"Great! The only reason I came to this stupid town was because Evangeline Cartwright agreed to be at this two-bit convention for crazy old cat ladies. I've been trying to interview her for the magazine. Uh, *Cat Lover*. If it hadn't been for her, I never would have signed up."

The next step in hotel etiquette would be for Nora to find Mr. Shaw an alternative place to stay somewhere close to the hotel. Her cantankerous customer was right. Piney Woods was a small town. His two remaining choices were Nora's home, which was the Piney Woods Bed and Breakfast, or a seedy motel on the highway called Hickelby's Motor Lodge. The thought of Allen Shaw staying with her at the bed and breakfast was not something she could deal with, even for a few days. Nora clicked off the details of staying at Hickleby's Motor Lodge like a telephone operator giving directory assistance. "There is a very economical place to stay, and it's right on the highway. You could get your interview and be out of town in no time." The idea of a brief visit for Mr. Shaw was wishful thinking on her part.

"Fine. What's the name of the hotel?"

"Hickelby's Motor Lodge. If you would like, I can give you their number and you can call them on your cell phone, or I could call and see if they have any rooms available."

"You're going to have to call. While taking the many planes I had to board to get to this godforsaken wilderness, I misplaced my phone."

Nora glanced at the number she had taped to the corner of the desk in case of emergencies and then dialed it. While she waited for old man Hickelby to answer his phone, she looked back at Alan Shaw. "Is it just you?"

"Just me." After her brief time with this man, it was no surprise that Mr. Shaw was traveling alone.

Mr. Hickelby answered on the sixth ring, a record for him. He was notorious for not answering the phone. That way, he kept his customer complaints to a minimum. He must have been sitting right by it.

"Hickelby's Motor Lodge. Stay for a day. Stay for an hour."

"Yes, Mr. Hickelby, I was wondering if you had any rooms available. We're booked up here at the Tunie."

"You're kidding me. The Tunie hasn't been fully booked in years. What are you doing? Are you giving your rooms away now?"

"No, we're actually charging. We have a convention in town this week, and we have a full house. Would you happen to have a room available?"

There was a pause on the other end, and Nora knew he was coming up with his room rate. It would be notably higher now.

"As it just so happens, my brother-in-law recently moved out. We have his room available."

If this was the brother-in-law Nora knew from around town, he was a heavy smoker. The Tunie didn't allow smoking in the rooms, but Bert Hickelby's motel was not as strict about that kind of thing.

"Excellent. I have a Mr. Alan Shaw, who will be renting your room. Hold on, and I'll let you speak with him."

As Mr. Shaw spoke and made the arrangements to rent the room, Nora looked up Evangeline Cartwright on the computer. She had seen her name on the promotional materials for the Meow Meetup but hadn't read the details. This lady wrote mystery novels that featured cats along with delightful, quirky characters in small town settings. They called them "cozy" mysteries. What a great idea.

Mr. Shaw handed back the phone. "I'm dropping my stuff over at Hickelby's, but I'll be back. Seeing as you have inconvenienced me so badly, I will expect to have a place to work here."

Nora gestured over to the new office center she and Max had constructed out of two-room dividers, some secondhand computers, and a fax machine. "We have our business area open now, and you're welcome to use that."

Shaw looked over and rolled his eyes. "Great. I'll bet that computer still connects to AOL through a phone modem. I hope you have enough floppy discs on hand," he said, his tone sarcastic. Mr. Shaw, who was Nora's first arrival for the convention, picked up his bags and stomped out the door.

Chapter 2

After getting Alan Shaw out of the lobby, Nora went through a laundry list that would make a wedding planner cry. She thought about the many tasks she had to perform before the convention guests descended on the Tunie. The first thing on her list was to deliver a bulky box of sheets to the fourth floor. These were the last few rooms they had remodeled to prepare for the convention, and some of the rooms hadn't been used in years. Nora and Marty had enjoyed choosing new sheets to match the warm colors they had put into the guest rooms. As Nora hoisted up the cardboard carton, a small woman whose glasses had slipped down her nose approached her, holding a brown mailing envelope.

"Excuse me, can you tell me if Evangeline Cartwright has arrived yet?" Her eyes, nearly free of makeup, were amplified slightly by thick lenses. She looked hopeful and a little giddy, something Nora would have associated with a young girl at a rock concert, even though the woman was probably in her forties.

Nora set down the box with a thud. "Not yet. Can I help you?"

"I was hoping she would be here already." Her gaze slipped to the floor, and she held the thick envelope closely. "My name is Izzy Franklin, and I work at the library."

"Nice to meet you."

"Thank you. It's nice to meet you. I'm a little embarrassed about why I'm here. I don't just check out books; I write them." The last part sounded like a confession, as if writing were some sort of subversive activity. Izzy Franklin held out the envelope and shook it slightly for emphasis. "Miss Cartwright is the world's best mystery writer, and, more than anything else, I want her to read my manuscript. I know it's presumptuous of me, but her being here is an opportunity I just can't pass up. I'm already late for work. Could you give her my manuscript when she arrives? All my contact information is inside, so if she wants to, she can call me day or night, on major holidays, or in the hospital."

This mouse of a woman handed off her precious envelope to Nora. It took a lot of nerve to part with something that had to be so very important. Nora wanted to do right by her. "Sure. I'd be glad to help." Nora took the envelope. "So, is this the next big bestseller?"

"Only Miss Cartwright can tell us that."

"I'll be sure to give it to her first thing when she arrives."

"Do you promise?"

Nora put a hand over her heart. "I promise." Then she winked. "Good luck, Izzy."

The aspiring writer smiled with a slight tremble on her bottom lip. "Thank you so much. This is all so exciting."

After Izzy left with a noticeable lift in her step, Nora added the thick envelope on top of the box of sheets as well as a file folder with her to-do list and the receipts that needed to be filed for the purchase of the sheets. The flaps of the box were not taped, so the manuscript slipped inside. Nora would have to retrieve it after she dropped off the sheets so that she could deliver it to Evangeline Cartwright. She lifted the large box again, letting it totter. She reached out to push the elevator button to ride up to the floor, where Jolene, the housekeeper, was waiting for the sheets. Under one of the tables was a stray petal from a fresh flower arrangement. Jolene was new to the job and didn't always have the diligence needed in clean a facility this large. The vacuuming was hitting the middle of the floor, but not under the tables or in the corner. Even though Nora had been against it, the Best of Show

Champion from the United States, a British Red Shorthair named Catpurnicas, would be attending but would be kept at a local kennel and would make an appearance on Saturday. The Tunie was lucky to get the convention in the first place. After making phone calls to many national organizations, Nora was surprised when the organizer agreed on their location. The Meow Meetup was a building block for future conventions. Starting with a cat convention might not sound impressive, but the hotel had been run down for so long that this gathering gave them all hope for a bright future.

Nora entered the ancient elevator and, reaching around the bulky cardboard box, her fingers mashed two buttons instead of one, causing the old elevator to stay still. She waited for the doors to close, but nothing was happening. She reached out again and hammered on the third-floor button, just in case the machinery wasn't sure which floor to take her to. Her phone rang as the doors began to close.

"Nora, I need to talk to you," Nora's uncle Wiley said on the other end. "We have a crisis here in the restaurant. We can't possibly feed these kitty lovers with the chicken that just came in. It's rancid. We're just lucky it smells so bad, or we might have ended up with a massive case of food poisoning. I don't know what we're going to do. It's not like we can find this much chicken at the Texas Star Market. We need to reorder, but there's no time. We'll never get it here and be able to marinate it and cook it by tomorrow night."

"Did you call the supplier?" The Tunie Hotel used Moore Foods Wholesale Supplier to restock food for the restaurant. Everyone who served food in Piney Woods used Moore Foods. Being in a small town, they had a monopoly on wholesale food delivery.

"Yes, I called them, but I had to leave a message. They are supposed to call me back." Nora worried when Uncle Wiley got stressed out. Wiley was a new member of the Alcoholics Anonymous 12-Step Program. The Meow Meetup convention had been a blessing for her, but as the manager of the Tunie Restaurant, it put her uncle under a tremendous amount of pressure. When Nora first met Wiley, he seemed to be drunk every day. Once he discovered Nora was his long-lost niece, he made a vow to her to straighten up his life. When he took over the restaurant, he promised to stay sober. So far, he has kept his word, but spoiled chicken and a restaurant full of hungry people could change everything. Recovering alcoholics so often are trying to live their newly formed lives on shaky foundations. Wiley was no different.

"Uncle Wiley, I'm heading upstairs right now because Jolene is having a fit about getting her hands on the new sheets that we ordered. As soon as I finish with her, I'll come to the restaurant, and we'll figure out what to do about the food situation. In the meantime, I want you to come up with an alternative dish in case we can't get our hands on some chicken."

"An alternative dish? But I have all the supplies for my special marinated chicken." His voice rose at the end, and she could tell he was not in a good way.

"Uncle Wiley, settle down. We'll work this out. They're not going to be here until tomorrow."

"Do you know how soon tomorrow is when you need to marinate?" he asked.

With a thud, the elevator jolted to a stop, knocking Nora to the floor. Wiley, not aware of the situation, continued his rant about the shortness of time and the chemistry of adding flavor to chicken through the process of marination. In the darkness of the stalled elevator, the only light in the metal box came from her cell phone.

Nora attempted to break into Wiley's panic attack. "Wiley! Uncle Wiley! Listen to me. I need your help."

"You need my help? I need yours. Good cookin' is a true art form, and without the proper ingredients..."

"Uncle Wiley, I need you to listen to me. The elevator stopped moving. I think I'm trapped."

"You're what?"

"The elevator was going, and then it stopped abruptly. The lights are out."

There was a silence on the other end, and then he spoke softly. "Are you okay?"

"I think so. It stopped so quickly it knocked me to the floor."

"I was supposed to be looking at that elevator. It's been right ornery lately, but I got so busy with the restaurant that I didn't get to it. I'm heading there now."

Uncle Wiley's side of the phone went dead. Nora attempted to stand, finding her way back to the button panel.

Her cell phone rang before she could finish the job. "Nora? Are you okay? Wiley just told me about the elevator." Her business partner, Marty, sounded tired but concerned. Getting ready for the convention must've been wearing her down as well.

"Yes, I'm okay," Nora assured her.

"We're going to call Max. He might be the night auditor, but you and I know if anybody can fix a machine, it would be him." Nora sighed. She knew Marty would want to call Max. She called him for everything. Unfortunately, his realm of knowledge was mainly the things he learned about computers after watching YouTube videos. "Marty, you know his expertise only applies to computers."

"Try to stay calm. If the elevator service can't get here for a day, then Max and Wiley will come up with a way to get you out of there."

"We have an elevator service?"

The budget at the Tunie was tighter than a divorcée's waistband on her first night back in the dating world. "No, but we'll find one. Hopefully, fixing it won't cost us a fortune. I guess I was taking too much of a risk trying to rely on Wiley to keep something as complicated as the elevator running."

Marty had been the one person who believed in Nora when she first came to town with a letter from her mother. Her arrival in Piney

Woods, Texas, was rough, but one of the first friends she made was Marty. Nora never forgot her kindness, and when she came into an inheritance, she knew she wanted to invest in Marty's pet project, the Tunie Hotel.

"Give us a little time. We'll call you again," Marty said before she ended the call.

Lonesome for company, Nora dialed another number.

"Lucy Cooper," Nora's half sister answered.

"Hey, Lucy, it's me."

"Hey girl, what are you up to?" Nora's mother as well as Lucy's mother had both fallen for the charms of Adam Brockwell, the man who saved the town from financial ruin after the oil bust. Nora's mother had been a young girl just out of high school, while Lucy's mother worked in Brockwell's house. He pursued them both, even while being married. Lucy, now a financial planner, used to work at the Piney Woods bank. She and her mother had decided to take a trip to New York City with some of her inheritance. Between the Broadway shows, jazz clubs, and shopping, they were having a wonderful time.

"Not much. I'm stuck in the elevator, and you?"

"We just spent the afternoon shopping on Fifth Avenue. Wait. What did you say? Dang. Are you serious?"

"Very."

"Lucky you, thanks to our daddy's inheritance, you're now half owner of that death trap. That elevator must be at least fifty years old. What can I do to help?"

"Do you know who the bank uses for maintenance on their elevator?"

"Not really, but Wilber at the bank always handled that kind of thing." There was a rustling in the background, and then Nora heard Lucy say, "That's beautiful. Do they have it in a size 7?" She then returned to the phone. "Can I call you back? We're shopping, and you won't believe the dress I just found." Lucy had a sense of style that just wouldn't stop. Nora had no doubt that she was buying out New York City.

"Sure, I'm not going anywhere," Nora answered.

"Yeah, right." There was a click on the other side.

Nora kicked off her shoes and sat down in a corner of the elevator, hugging her knees to her chest. Was there any possibility that the cables on the elevator could break? Had they ever been replaced during their decades of use? By her estimation, she was somewhere around the second floor. Even though she hadn't always agreed with her mother, this was one time she would have loved to hear her reassuring voice, telling her everything was going to be all right. The sound of the cell phone cut through the air.

"Nora?"

She breathed in a sigh of relief as she recognized the low male voice on the other end. "Hi, Tuck."

"Marty told me about the elevator. Are you hurt?" Tuck's sweet words were a balm to Nora's sense of aloneness as she sat on the floor in the dark.

"Don't worry, Wiley and Max are on it," Nora assured him.

"And me," Tuck added. "You have me." The police department, where Tuck was an officer, was right next to the Tunie Hotel, so he wasn't too far away. She loved the sound of his voice, and lately, she had come to the delightful conclusion that she was in love with the rest of him, too. From the unevenness of his breath, she could tell he was walking.

"I'm in the hotel now. I see Wiley. Hold on." Nora heard muffled voices, and then Tuck returned to the line. "We're going to try to force open the doors on the third floor, and hopefully the elevator car is somewhere close. Do you see any light from the crack in the door?"

Near the ceiling, there was a sliver of light illuminating the tiny line where the doors met. "Yes. I see it. I see the light." Her words sounded like a bad line in a cheesy horror movie. Then again, being stuck in an elevator in a very old hotel was also kind of like being in a slasher flick.

"We're going to try to open the doors and see if we can get you out that way. Just hold tight. Don't go anywhere."

Where was she going to go? Sitting quietly in the dark, she could just make out the voices of Wiley and Tuck above her. They were going to get her out, she was sure, but that nagging little thought about the elevator cable breaking was starting to surface. She again tried to calculate the bodily damage that would occur when she suddenly shot to the bottom. She was just above the second floor, which meant there had to be about a 25-foot drop. Then she went a step further with her anxiety and thought about what would happen to the Meow Meetup convention if they didn't have a working elevator. Many of the cat fanciers were older people. The thought of climbing stairs to get to their room at night could be catastrophic. She giggled to herself. *Cat* astrophic.

Why was she giggling? Maybe the oxygen in the elevator was growing thin? She'd probably be passed out by the time Tuck and Wiley pulled her out. She started breathing deeper, thinking if she could get more oxygen to her brain, she'd stop acting like an idiot. There was a giant creak as Tuck and Wiley grunted against the door. Nora waited for the sliver of light to widen, but nothing was happening.

Wiley came onto Tuck's phone. "So, Nora," Wiley said, his words even and modulated as if speaking to a small child. "These old elevators are a piece of work, but we have the door open. For some reason, the fourth floor seems to be stuck open, too. Max is here now, and he has an idea. I'll give him the phone."

There was a shuffling of the phone, and Max came on the line. "Hey, Nora. You just love to wake me up from my sleep, don't you?" At over three hundred pounds, Nora had worried about Max manning the hotel by himself all night. Marty lived in the hotel, and there had been many nights when Nora finished her shift and found Marty and Max talking as old friends do. Their friendship had spanned decades.

"Here's my plan, Nora. It all depends on you. Look up at the ceiling. One of those tiles should be a door to the shaft. You need to open it."

Nora's breathing stopped. If he was having her find a passageway, he was going to tell her to lift herself into the elevator shaft.

When she didn't respond right away, Max asked, "Are you listening?"

"Yes."

"Good girl. So, you're going to climb out of that door and get on the little ladder that's on the wall of the shaft. That ladder is going to lead to the door that's open on the third floor. All you have to do is climb the ladder."

Nora looked at the tiles above her and put the phone on speaker and into her pocket. Four squares covered the ceiling. She remembered that three had lights and one did not. More than likely, that was where the door was. She put the box of sheets squarely under it.

"Do you have the tile off?"

"No," she answered sharply. Didn't he realize she had to process this information and then get enough guts up to actually do it? "I'm about to try it." She refolded the top flaps of the box to give it more strength. One of the flaps caught on the brown mailing envelope that held Izzy Franklin's manuscript, causing it to rip. Right now, that couldn't concern her. Hoping that the box of sheets did not collapse under her weight, she stepped up gingerly. Once her footing was steady, she pushed on the ceiling tile and found herself staring into the elevator shaft. There was a ray of light coming through the open door on the third floor.

"I have the ceiling tile off," she shouted up into the darkness.

The circle of a flashlight beam roamed across the elevator shaft. "Great!" Max said. "If you can pull up on that cross bar on the top of the elevator, that will put you into the shaft. Find the ladder. Get on that and take a few steps toward me."

The thought of climbing on top of an elevator car terrified Nora. Her hands shook as she gripped the crossbar. Pulling her entire body weight upward with her arms felt impossible. "I can't do it."

Marty cheered her on, her voice echoing in the shaft. "You can do it, Nora. Try one more time."

Tuck's voice joined Marty's. "See if you can jump up."

If she did that, she took the chance of the cardboard box collapsing under her. She wasn't a large woman, but she could break cardboard. Drawing in a breath, she counted and made a jump for the bar. She pulled her elbows over the rail, then dragged a leg up into the elevator shaft. Once she got on top, she took a second and rested. Spotting the ladder on the wall, Nora felt a surge of relief. The only problem was that her view included the perilous way down to the first floor.

"Don't look down. Just grab hold of the ladder," Wiley shouted.

Easy for him to say, she thought. Nora pulled herself up and started climbing the ladder, trying not to look at the cement tunnel that could lead to her death. After a couple of steps up, she felt strong arms pulling her out of the elevator shaft and onto the carpet of the third floor.

"Are you okay?" Tuck asked. Nora knocked the dust and grime from the elevator off her blue silk dress. She had loved the color and purchased it with the convention in mind. Now it looked bedraggled and stained.

"Except for a little grease, I seem to be just fine. I'm afraid I left some paperwork—the new sheets and an envelope for Evangeline Cartwright—in the elevator."

"That's okay. I'll take care of it later when we get the elevator fixed," Marty assured her.

Pulling her to her feet, Wiley shook his head. "It was on my list. I knew I should have gotten to this. There is just so much going on with the restaurant right now. It's my fault." Wiley pulled a small plastic coin out of his pocket. "It's my six-month chip from Alcoholics Anonymous. At this rate, I'm not sure if I'm going to make it to my next one."

Nora agreed that the chance of a back slide was significantly increasing. Her phone rang in her pocket.

"You wouldn't believe this. I just picked up a Kate Spade purse for forty-five dollars. They were selling it right on the street. I had no idea they had street boutiques. Are you still stuck?" Lucy asked.

"I'm out. Thanks, and I would check inside that bag to see if it's a knock-off. A street boutique? I thought you were the investment counselor."

"Counselor, yes, big city savvy, maybe not so much. Dang, I'll bet the guy doesn't have a return policy either."

"I'm guessing no."

"I'm so glad I have you to look out for me. You should be careful and stay out of rickety elevators. You're the only white half sister I have," Lucy said.

Nora ended the call and turned to Wiley. "Don't worry about it, Uncle Wiley. Let me take care of the elevator. You keep working on the chicken."

"Better yet, let me," Marty said. "You worry about the front desk. I'll work on the elevator."

Tuck, who had been staring up the shaft looking for God knows what, now returned to the group. "What a way to start your day, sweetheart. Are you sure you're okay?" He took her hand in his, warmly enclosing it.

Nora was young and fit, but crawling out of an elevator had been tough for her. Just one more thing to worry about before the cat lovers descended on them.

"I'm out of that elevator now, so no worries." Nora squeezed his hand. As she drew closer to Tuck, Max lumbered backward to get out of her way. In the process, he stepped on Marty's foot, and she twisted around to be free. When she did, her ankle twisted, and she landed on the floor.

"Are you all right?" Nora asked.

Max's chin quivered. "Oh gosh, Marty. I'm so sorry. I stepped on you with my big clodhopper of a foot." He reached for her hand to help her unsteadily to her feet.

"Uh," she said, putting her hand on Max's arm. "I think I'm okay." She tried to take a step, but then her foot faltered.

"You are not okay, and it's all my fault. Let's get some ice on that." Max said, taking charge.

"Nora, we need to get on that elevator." Marty said through clenched teeth.

"Lucy told me to call Wilber at the bank. He should have the elevator guy's name on file."

"Good. I'll call Wilber about the elevator from my apartment, and then I think I'm going to put my foot up."

"Are you sure you don't want to just leave it to me?" Max said. He was now in hover mode around Marty.

"No. I'm fine. It will take five minutes."

"If you say so," Max said, eyeing her cautiously as he helped Marty limp toward the stairway.

Tuck grabbed Nora's other hand. "You scared me. Try not to do that again today, okay? I know you have a lot going on with the convention, and I'm trying to stay out of your way, but I can be over here in a heartbeat." Tuck kissed her lightly but lingered enough that Nora gently pushed him away.

"And I love knowing that. Now head back to the police station. I have to get back to work."

Chapter 3

Her thoughts still dwelling in Tuck's goodbye kiss, Nora's mood was renewed, and she returned to the lobby to find Max standing at the computer.

"She's upstairs. That ankle is swelling up. I know this is terrible timing, but Marty is going to need to stay off it for at least a day or two. With or without her, I'd say it's system go for the countdown."

"I can't believe the convention is finally here, and we've lost Marty."

"I know what you mean." He picked up the phone. "Let me just give her a call and make sure she's really staying off that foot. She can be stubborn, you know." Max spoke into the phone and punched the intercom button. "Are you okay up there? Do we need to send up some ice?"

"I'm fine," she assured him. "I took some ibuprofen, and the throbbing has started to go away."

Nora added, "Really, we can send up a bucket of ice."

"No thanks. I can't believe I did this. You wouldn't happen to have any gossip magazines and boxed chocolates, would you? I'm ready to wallow in despair right now."

As Max hung up the phone, a look of concern crossed his face. "She's going to go stir crazy up there. We need to make sure she stays off that foot."

Wiley slunk into the lobby with guilt written all over him. Nora turned to her uncle, whose shoulders were sagging on his thin frame.

"You told me that the elevator was acting up, but I didn't know it was that bad."

Wiley looked down at his fingernails. "I'm so sorry. I know I should have gotten to it. I have the elevator car down to the first floor now, but I wouldn't recommend anybody using it until we get a repairman here. I've just been so busy with the restaurant. It's one thing to give an old drunk management of a restaurant, but it's quite another to tell him to feed a herd of cat lovers in one weekend. It's a lot on a guy."

He was right. It was a lot of responsibility to put on one man. If he hadn't been her mother's brother, would she have jumped into giving management of the Tunie restaurant to a lifelong alcoholic? There was a reason why people checked in and out of rehab like it was a revolving door. Stress can knock any resolution out the window, no matter how heartfelt.

"Don't worry about the elevator. You're right. I'm putting too much on you. I'm fine, and we're working on fixing it."

Wiley's assistant cook, Caesar, now stood behind them, holding a dish towel in his hands. His white cook's jacket clung a little tightly around his waist. "Wiley, we have a problem."

"What now?" Wiley asked, running his hands through his thinning hair.

"Moore Foods just put our beef patties on back order. We're going to run out of hamburgers." Nora's eyes widened. Was Moore Foods trying to drive them out of business?

Wiley shook his head. "Then find somebody who can get them to us today."

"There's no one. Right now, the only supply company that delivers to Piney Woods is Moore Foods."

"If you need to get into your car and drive to the grocery store, do it. I'll get to the kitchen as soon as I can, and we'll try to sort this thing out, but the first thing I have to do is find someone to fix the elevator."

"I told you, there is no need to do that, Uncle Wiley. Lucy has someone for us. You just worry about the restaurant, okay?"

Usually, Nora worked five to eleven, but with the convention being her baby, she volunteered to work double shifts for the event. The hours were exhausting, but what else could she do? She wanted to make the Tunie Hotel successful again. The Tunie had been the place to be in Piney Woods, Texas, from the forties to the eighties. When Mr. Tunie died, it fell into disrepair and was about to be closed for good when Marty picked it up for a dime in a foreclosure sale. Now that Nora was co-owner, reviving the Tunie had become her life, and if that meant helping old ladies up the stairs for the next two days, she would do it.

"Oh, my God," Max said from the front desk.

"What? Is something wrong with the software?"

"Worse." His blue eyes widened as the screen reflected on them.

"What could be worse than the only technology we have going down before our first big convention?"

"We received a one-star review on Rate Your Hotel."

"Huh? What's that?" Nora asked.

"It's a hotel review service. It's been gaining popularity in the last year. You can search the name of a hotel you're thinking about booking and see what other people thought of it first."

"Oh yeah. They have sites like that for restaurants, too," Wiley said. "Stuff like that can put you out of business."

"One star? What did the guest say was wrong?" The Tunie Hotel usually booked from one-half to three-fourths of their rooms. Being newly reopened, they tried to give first-rate service and hospitality. Nora searched her memory for any upset guests.

"Wow. Everything," Max read on. "Bad location, bad service, a smell, and cockroaches crawling everywhere. Oh, no."

"This can't be good, Nora," Wiley said.

Max gasped again.

"Max?" Nora asked.

"We just went from one review to ten, all by the same person. They're popping up all over. All one star. Whoever is doing this is doing it right now. I can't believe they didn't limit the reviewer."

"People will figure out this is some crackpot, and that will be the end of it," Nora rationalized.

"If it were only that way. Even if those ten reviews were by one person, it makes our overall average one star. It's going to take a lot of five-star reviews to bring up our score on this site."

Nora had only been in the hotel business for a brief time. "Maybe we should call Marty?"

Max shook his head. "I don't know. What she needs right now is to stay off that ankle, not another crisis." Max's protectiveness toward Marty was touching.

"I guess we could wait," Nora said.

Max nodded. "Just for a while."

Nora turned slightly toward Max. "Can I ask you something?"

"Shoot."

"Are you and Marty, you know, interested in each other?"

Wiley held up a hand. "I've got to get back to the restaurant. You two can talk about your love lives and spare me."

As Wiley made a quick exit, Max's face turned a deep shade of pink, highlighting his rounded cheeks. "It depends on who you are asking. I didn't know I was that transparent." He blinked, looked down, and lowered his voice. "From the time we were kids working here for Mr. Tunie, I have always had a special place in my heart for Marty."

"Why didn't you ever act on it?"

Max jerked his head back slightly. "Have you looked at me lately?" He threw his arms down around his wide girth like a clumsy ballet dancer. "Marty is beautiful. Sleek. A businesswoman. I'm this overweight guy who lives with his mother and studies for his law degree online. I have no idea why she hasn't married up until now, but she's never looked my way. I'm not much of a catch."

"That is not true. Well, the part about living with your mother and trying to become a lawyer is true. Your outside might be big, but so is your incredible heart. You are one of the kindest, sweetest men I've ever met. Anybody would be lucky to get you."

"And there is, oh, so much of me to get," Max added, sarcasm in his voice.

"Okay, fine. You're worried about your size. You know, there are a lot of excellent fashions out there for big and tall men these days. Why don't you snazz up your look? Just because you're Grande doesn't mean you can't look grand."

Max listened, his eyes sliding to the side as he considered Nora's idea. Nora continued, "What about Marty? You tell me how perfect she is. Don't you think a woman with that many redeeming qualities would judge a good friend because of his size?"

"Friend. That's the word. I not only live in the friend zone, but I have my own subdivision."

Nora put her hands on her hips and planted her feet as she looked up at Max's blue eyes. "I think you should go for it."

"Are you serious?"

"Yes. Nothing ventured."

"No way. If I were to tell Marty I think about her day and night and wish we could be together, it could ruin the friendship we have now. That is too much to risk. As much as I appreciate your advice to the lovelorn, we need to work on those one-star reviews." Max and Marty's friendship was a wonderful thing to observe, and Nora could understand Max's not wanting to take a risk.

An attractive older woman with dark blond hair styled in a short cut stood walked up to the counter. "Oh, I know all about one-star reviews. They're the plight of any endeavor." She wore a tweed skirt and a matching beige camel-hair jacket. Nora immediately recognized her from the banner in the lobby advertising the Meow Meetup convention. This was Evangeline Cartwright, the famous mystery writer, who was the keynote speaker and the main draw for the gathering.

"Miss Cartwright!" Nora tried holding her hand over the grease stain left from climbing out of the elevator. "How nice to meet you."

Evangeline's smile was warm. She might have achieved notoriety in her field, but there was a very friendly feeling about her. "I hope you don't mind, but I'm a little early. I like to get to know a place before I speak. It takes away some of the nervousness."

Nora scooted behind the front desk, bumping into Max. "That's quite all right. We're honored to have you here."

Evangeline looked around the ancient walls of the Tunie. The wallpaper in the main lobby had been restored to the original print that had been there in 1945. Large chandeliers sparkled, reflecting light on the highly polished wood. "What an interesting old place. No matter what your sour apple of a reviewer said on the computer, I'll bet there are some stories to tell around here."

While Max checked Evangeline's reservation, Nora replied, "Yes. The Tunie has been here since the forties. If you look closely at that wall, you'll find pictures not only of the generations of visitors and townspeople of Piney Woods but a few celebrities like LBJ and Waylon Jennings." In Texas, these two well-known gentlemen were ranked at the same level of honor.

Evangeline stepped over and examined the vast collection of photographs collected by Mr. Tunie over the years. "This is incredible. Would you mind if I snapped some pictures of them later? Your wall of visitors is a tremendous bank of potential characters for my next novel."

"We don't mind at all," Nora assured her. "You'll be taking a picture of my own mother up there. Again, it's quite an honor having you here." Nora was especially proud that they had started a section of new pictures, beginning with a panorama shot of the reunion she and Marty had held just recently.

"Oh, I want to make sure to remember this one," Evangeline said as she leaned closer to a picture of a tall, thin man. Nora didn't recognize him, but the novelist liked his photograph. What would he turn out to be in her novel?

"Miss Cartwright, our elevator is not working right now. How are you with stairs? We put you on the fourth floor, thinking it would give you the most privacy. If the stairs are a problem, we can put you on the first floor."

"And bump somebody else? Nothing doing. I walk three miles a day. The older you get, the more important it is to exercise. I certainly think I can handle a few stairs."

Her statement gave Nora tremendous relief. If the rest of the guests had this attitude, she might be able to sleep at night. Evangeline Cartwright had drifted over to the pamphlet rack and picked up a few of the three-fold brochures that advertised the town's attractions. "You have a lovely little town. I hope I can get some time to sightsee a bit."

"Thank you, and I agree. People don't always think of East Texas as a vacation destination, which makes finding it even better."

Pocketing a couple of brochures in her spacious quilted bag, she returned to the desk. "Would you happen to have a map of the city?" Most people pull up maps on their phones these days, but the writer was from a different generation. Nora pulled out a few she kept on hand for non-computer-savvy customers.

"Thank you. And is there a phone book nearby?" Again, not the usual request. Nora pulled a weathered phone book out from behind the counter and dusted it off.

"Thank you again. Oh, and I was wondering if you could do me a little favor. I'd like to get accustomed to the place, so if anybody asks for me, tell them I'm checking in right before the conference."

On top of the tattered, neglected phone book, Nora placed the key to Evangeline's room. "No problem. Like I said, you're on the top floor, right next to one of the owners of the Tunie."

"Just one?"

"You're looking at the other," Nora beamed.

"Well then, it's nice to meet you." She looked for Nora's nametag.

"Nora. Nora Alexander."

With the arrival of her delightful keynote speaker for the convention, the elevator breaking and disparaging review didn't seem to matter as much. No matter what, the Tunie would keep going. A few hours later, Nora was in the office going through preparations for the convention the next day. Jolene walked in and plopped the file folder of hotel receipts on the desk Nora had been carrying before getting trapped in the elevator.

"Here ya go. These dogs are pooped," she said, pointing to her feet clad in discount store sneakers. Nora smiled. Jolene had been one of Tuck's rescues after he put her husband in jail for selling drugs. Tuck was good at that. Rescuing.

After Jolene left, Nora decided to call and check on Marty. Her voice was faint on the other end. "Did I wake you?" Nora asked.

"No. I'm too bored to sleep. Most of my day has been spent watching the colors change on my ankle."

"Maybe we should get you in for an x-ray?"

"No. I think it's just a sprain. I've sprained this ankle before and broken bones. I can tell the difference. I'm fine, really."

"Are you sure I can't get you something?"

"No, but thanks for asking. How is it going?"

"Jolene just left. I'm worried about all the people coming tomorrow. I hope we can handle it. Know any Boy Scouts looking for a merit badge?"

"Max is the only Boy Scout I know. Dominic comes in a little later. He said he couldn't work this morning because he was sleeping off a paranormal investigation that he and a couple of buddies conducted over at the old mill." Dominic Fazio, a transplanted New Yorker, was a new hire at the Tunie Hotel. Marty and Nora assigned him to the front desk. He then informed them that his job that would pay the bills would be working the Tunie, but the passion of his life was being a paranormal investigator. With the Tunie Hotel having its long history and possible ghost sightings, it was an ideal position for him.

"Good Lord, not another investigation. Dear old Max, what would we do without him?" Marty sighed. Nora noted the tenderness in her voice when she mentioned Max. Maybe she was right, and it did seem like there might be something there. After her discussion with Max, she had to ask.

"So, you and Max. Were you ever a couple?"

Marty paused as she considered the question. "Max? No. I guess I depend on him for everything, but we were never a couple. We've known each other since high school, but I was on the cheer squad, and he was in the debate club. We met working here in the summer, and Mr. Tunie decided to have a Hawaiian theme. Max and I were in charge of decorating the lobby. I never laughed so hard. He was just so funny, you know? We even had hula dancers in the front lobby one night. Max and I had so much fun that summer, but when school began again, I went back to the popular crowd, and he went back to the debate team. Funny, though. All those beautiful people, the football players, and the prom queens aren't a part of my life anymore. Max is. I guess he always will be." Her tone grew wistful. She seemed like a put-together businesswoman, but for a second, she was that popular girl who ran with all the right people in high school.

"I should get off the phone and let you rest. If you need anything, just call."

"Sure. Don't forget, I have the webcam focused on the lobby. You're doing a wonderful job. It's not as if you don't have anything else to do. Don't worry about me; just keep the hotel up and running."

Nora felt bad for not telling Marty about the reviews some creep was posting about the Tunie as she replaced the phone in the cradle. Before it could overwhelm her, she set herself back to the tasks at hand.

Nora lifted the tan folder and looked underneath it. She had expected to find Izzy's manuscript, but it was not with the file. It had to still be in the box with the sheets, and those sheets would've been taken out and put on the beds by now. Why hadn't Jolene delivered them both to the office? What if Izzy's manuscript was lost? She had spoken to Evangeline earlier and had forgotten all about it. All she could hope was that she put it in a safe place somewhere and not in the trash. She was a little on the sketchy side, but so far she had been reliable and took instructions well. If she lost Izzy's manuscript, it was like not returning a library book late. She thought of the little woman with the thick glasses. She was depending on Nora to help her pursue her dream of becoming a published author. With her luck, Jolene dumped the envelope in the trash.

Chapter 4

"Hey beautiful. Up for some dinner? I know a nice little place right here in the hotel." Tuck leaned against the doorway and his very presence provided a welcome escape from the pre-convention anxiety she was feeling. She would find the manuscript after she had dinner with Tuck. She would be able to think more clearly.

"Yes!" Nora quickly put down the folder, rose from the desk and went into Tuck's arms. His kiss started out light, but when he caught her eagerness, he lengthened their embrace.

When they finally pulled apart, he spoke, his voice low. "Well, hello."

"You're like a port in a storm. Dinner sounds wonderful but then I have to get my mind back on the hotel. I still don't feel ready."

"Did you get Wiley's chicken problem straightened out?"

"We're working on it."

"Somehow, I knew that you would. What's he serving tonight?"

"I don't know. I'm starved. How about you? Let's go see. I haven't seen him pacing the floor in a while so maybe things are better with him."

He slipped his arm around her waist and guided her to the door. "I think we're Wiley's most frequent diners."

"I believe you might be right. Lucky for us we both like gumbo," Nora said.

"And each other," Tuck whispered. This was the way it had been between them for months. Nora loved having Tuck around and he seemed to feel the same. If it kept up like this, who knows where it would lead?

When Tuck and Nora stepped into the doorway of the restaurant, Evangeline Cartwright was already seated at a table with an older gentleman deep in conversation. His hair was a mixture of gray and black and his athletic build would've qualified him to be a spokesperson for a prescription drug company. Nora crossed her arms and whispered to Tuck, "Would you look at that. It seems Miss Evangeline has found a new friend."

"I think I recognize that guy," Tuck said, eyeing him. They walked over to the table in the corner and took a seat. Tuck glanced at the keynote speaker and her date. "How old is Evangeline Cartwright?"

"She's got to be between sixty-five and seventy."

Tuck laughed, "I guess she's a mover and shaker in more than just writing novels."

"I'll be right back," Nora said rising from the table. She returned shortly with her cell phone and pulled up the camera function.

"You can't do that," Tuck whispered. "It's an invasion of her privacy."

"Mr. Tunie would have wanted me to take this picture for his wall. She's a celebrity. I will ask her if it is okay. I think we have a little room next to Mattress Mack, the furniture guy from Houston who gave up his million-dollar showroom for Hurricane Harvey refugees." Nora quickly snapped the picture and pocketed the phone.

Tuck shook his head at her. He picked up the menu. "Wonder if Wiley has updated the menu?"

"I have to know the story behind that guy." Nora grabbed Tuck's hand and dragged him to Evangeline's table. "Hello there, are you enjoying your dinner?"

"Yes, we are," Evangeline answered as she dabbed at the corner of her mouth with a napkin.

"I was wondering if I could take your picture for our wall of fame?"

The gentleman sitting next to Evangeline stood up. "Wonderful idea. I'll just move out of the way, so you can capture our honored author." As Nora snapped the picture with her phone, Evangeline's dinner date said, "I haven't been to the hotel since it's been remodeled. It's wonderful you brought the restaurant back. This is a treat."

Tuck pointed a finger at Evangeline's dinner guest. "You look so familiar. I've seen you around town."

"Probably so. I get in quite often. I'm Doug Lindstrom. I own the dog kennel out on Barnes Road. I am also housing your celebrity show cat for the convention, Catpurnicus. They'll be bringing him in tomorrow." He extended an arm to shake Tuck's hand and flicked off a little piece of white fuzz that was resting on the sleeve of his navy-blue sweater. "Sorry about that. We also offer dog grooming, and lately we've had a run on white poodles."

Nora leaned a little closer as Doug Lindstrom shook Tuck's hand. "Are you sure you want to be hanging out with all these cat people this weekend?"

"Not a problem. Especially if I get to be in the company of the lovely Evangeline."

"How do you two know each other?" Tuck asked.

"Doug is a fan of my books. He's been writing to me for years and with the opportunity of being this close, I decided we should finally meet."

"That's so romantic," Nora put her hands together to the side of her face imitating an old-fashioned swoon.

"Miss Cartwright?" said a voice from behind them. Izzy Franklin held her hands in front almost in prayer as she surveyed her writing hero. "Is it really you?"

"Yes," Evangeline answered somewhere between friendly and cautious.

"I'm a writer too," she said stepping forward. "Did you get my manuscript?"

Evangeline looked puzzled, but before Nora could try to explain, Alan Shaw, the pushy reporter, pushed his bulk past Izzy causing her to knock over a chair. "Isn't this interesting? Who do we have here? Evangeline Cartwright and obviously an old friend. Could this be someone we should all get to know better?"

Doug stood up, tossing his napkin on the table. "Can I help you sir? Miss Cartwright and I are having dinner and would appreciate some privacy."

"Yes, I bet you would," the reporter laughed. "Privacy is so important to people like you. I have a few questions I don't think you're going to like." Evangeline gasped.

"Excuse me sir, I must ask you to leave," Doug said, his voice in a low but businesslike tone.

"I'm sure you'd like that now wouldn't you. You would just hate to cause a scene. You would hate to have everybody from the restaurant look over. If there were only more people here. Of course, what would you expect in a place like Piney Woods, Texas? I think I know who you are, sweetie," Shaw shouted.

Wiley stepped out of the kitchen when the reporter's voice was loud enough to be heard throughout the restaurant.

"What's the problem here?" Tuck asked.

"There's no problem. It's a free country and if I want to sit, say at this table, you can't stop me." Alan Shaw pulled out a chair at the table right next to Evangeline's.

"Mr. Shaw, I will not have you harassing my guests," Nora said.

Wiley crossed his arms and spoke in a forcefully quiet tone. "You'd better move, fella. Her boyfriend's the fuzz. She can put him on your trail with the crook of her finger." Wiley walked over and placed his hand under Shaw's elbow. Tuck did the same to the other side, and they escorted the interloper out.

"You haven't heard the last of me. I already took down this hotel today and now I'm shooting for you. I'm almost sure who you are. If I only had a DNA test handy, then I could prove it," Alan Shaw shouted as he was dragged from the restaurant.

"Thank you," Doug said, returning to his seat.

"Man, he must love his work, getting this excited about writing about an author of cat mysteries," Nora said. "After that little outburst, I think we can deduce who our internet troll is. I'll bet we can trace every single one of those bad reviews back to him."

Izzy, who had regained standing had been quiet watching the whole scene. "He should never have been so rude, Miss Cartwright. I'm glad they threw him out. You are so much more than an author of cat mysteries. You're my inspiration. My life's blood." Izzy Franklin adjusted her glasses and then placed her hands over her heart. Nora worried she was about to swoon.

"That's very kind of you," Evangeline said. "I don't know if I'm all that."

Tuck returned from the lobby.

Doug patted her hand. "Of course, you are, my dear."

He glanced toward the doorway. "Does this type of thing happen often? I had no idea the world of cat mysteries was so dangerous."

"It's not. This fellow just seemed to think he was hot on the trail of something. What that was, I have no idea," Evangeline said with a ready smile.

"He was way out of line and should never have been allowed into the hotel." Doug cast an angry glance Nora's way.

"Stop now," Evangeline said, laying a hand on Doug's arm. She glanced up at Izzy. "I would love to hear about your book."

"You would?"

"Of course, I would, and I promise not to steal the plot."

Nora knew this was the moment to come clean. "About your manuscript. We had some difficulty with our elevator, and I ended up having to climb out of it. That being said, your manuscript was left in the elevator with a box of sheets."

"You left my manuscript?" Izzy looked hurt, as if Nora had left behind her kindergarten-aged child.

"I did, but I was trying to climb into an elevator shaft. It would have been worse if all your pages scattered while I was trying to hold onto the ladder. You understand, don't you? I'm very sorry, but I promise I will get it to Evangeline as soon as we can access the elevator again."

"Never you mind," Evangeline said. "Tell me about what you've written. I trust Nora here to get it to me."

Izzy clumsily pulled a chair over causing Doug to scoot away from her. "You see, it starts on a dark and stormy night ..." Izzy was in heaven retelling her story and her eyes grew bright as she soaked in Evangeline's attention. Nora and Tuck quietly returned to their corner table. Evangeline Cartwright was a real class act. As Evangeline's eyes were focused on Izzy, brightening at plot points giving the rookie writer encouragement, Doug's eyes were focused on her. He seemed like so much more than a fan.

Chapter 5

The next morning, Nora ate a bowl of cereal at the breakfast table of the Piney Woods B&B. Nora watched Tatty at the stove, frying eggs. Ed was immersed in his newspaper. They both could have easily slipped into retirement, but buying the house they now lived in and turning it into a bed and breakfast had been Tatty's dream. With the Tunie Hotel becoming run down and then going through a lengthy renovation process and being the only other place in town owned by Bert Hickelby, the little B&B did good business. Even with the Tunie reopening, they still enjoyed full bookings.

"You're going to need your protein today, Chica. Those people at the hotel will run you ragged." Tatty slid two fried eggs onto a plate, added a piece of buttered toast, and placed it all at the table in front of Nora.

"I know. Thanks for making me breakfast. This is so much better than my cereal."

"Cereal. Phew." Ed folded down his newspaper. "You can't tell it from the cardboard box it comes in." He pointed to his plate. "This right here is real food. I just hope those goofy cat people upstairs don't smell it and think they're getting it." Ed used the term real food as if he were letting Nora in on some sort of rare treasure. Tatty had laid out a buffet of waffles, fresh fruit, and gooey pecan muffins in the dining room for the two guests they had gained from the Meow Meetup convention. It was delicious food and the kind of stuff people from the city expected when they were roughing it in Texas.

Nora had been living at the bed and breakfast for almost a year now. She loved her sunny yellow room that looked out onto the street. When she first came to town, she was practically penniless after the death of her mother. Now, Nora had a family she had never known about and money she had never expected to inherit. Eventually, she planned to find a house, but until then, Ed and Tatty had become her unofficial family. Their home had become hers, even with the motley assortment of weekend bed and breakfast boarders. All the other visitors ate in the dining room, while she ate in the kitchen.

"When will most of the convention goers be checking in?" Tatty asked.

"Around eleven or so. The first function is the cocktail party at four, so once they check in, they'll have the afternoon to get comfortable. With the elevator being out of order, I dread carrying those bags up the stairs."

Ed gingerly touched his back. "You'd know I'd help you if I could."

"I just hope everything is still standing when we have the anniversary party." Tatty and Ed had scheduled their party in the banquet room last year. That was before the Meow Meetup was even on the books. Nora had been so excited when they chose the Tunie for their anniversary party. At the time, she thought it might be the biggest function they had there all year. That was before she achieved the goal of getting an official convention to use the facilities at the Tunie Hotel.

"Wear comfortable shoes. You're going to get a workout." Tatty turned toward her husband. "And Ed, don't think you're getting out of chores today because you can put your hand on your back and wince a little," she added, giving him assurances that he had not fooled her.

As Nora drove the two blocks to work, a large delivery truck was slowing down in front of Jumbo Gumbos, the Tunie restaurant's main competition. Jumbo Gumbo specialized in gumbo but also all kinds of

Cajun food, including crawfish étouffée and Po Boy sandwiches. Being this close to the Louisiana border, Cajun dishes with French names were very popular with the citizens of Piney Woods.

There was no love lost between the two businesses, especially since Nora had taken Jumbo Gumbo's head cook and hired him to work at the Tunie. It was her uncle's talent that made Jumbo Gumbo financially solvent in the last few years. Now that Wiley was gone, the owner, Jumbo Jim, had returned to running the restaurant and was desperate to bring in customers.

The white truck with the name Moore Foods painted in green on the side pulled into the alley behind the restaurant. Nora knew that this would be an excellent opportunity to make sure that the truck was on its way to the hotel after his present delivery. She parked across the street at the hotel and then walked around the back of the delivery truck. The driver, a burly man in his thirties with a scruffy beard, was dressed in a standard gray shirt and a pair of shorts. He was handing boxes from the back of the refrigerated truck to a dolly that he would deliver to the kitchen. Jumbo Jim was a heavyset man, with the majority of his weight in the front. He stood with his hands placed on his hips as he watched the delivery driver hoist each box onto the dolly.

"Excuse me?" The two men didn't respond but seemed to be wrapped up in the process of unloading the boxes. "Excuse me?" Nora repeated and walked around until she was in full view of the driver, who then stopped.

The driver tipped his ball cap at Nora. His eyes went from friendly to leering. "Good morning, beautiful." He smacked his lips at her.

"Good morning. I'm one of the owners of the Tunie Hotel and was just checking to make sure you have a delivery for us this morning," Nora said, ignoring his tone.

"Little Missy, I heard something about that. My truck's almost empty, though. Let me check with my dispatcher to see when you will be getting your food." The driver hitched a leg up in the cab of the truck and got on a handheld radio, the yellow cord swirling down onto the seat. "Hey, Beth, I was wondering if you could look up the order for the Tunie? When will that be delivered?" He listened and then began to nod. Her voice was garbled on the other end, and he leaned forward into the cab of the truck to hear her. Once she finished speaking, he hopped down to Nora. "The soonest we'll be able to get anything over there would be around noon. That do you?"

Nora searched her memory to make sure she had the time right. "Noon? I thought you were delivering our food this morning."

"You people think you can put in a last-minute order, but it just don't work that way. Don't worry, sweetheart, we'll sure try to get it to you," the driver reassured her. "Thanks, Beth," he said back into the handheld radio.

Jumbo Jim glanced at the delivery driver, and the two of them exchanged a look Nora couldn't quite make out. Whatever it was, it didn't make her feel comfortable. "You even have that place up and running?" Jim asked, his heavy eyebrows slanting into his eyes. He didn't even try to hide his cynicism.

"For quite a while, thank you. But of course, you already know that from the smaller crowds you've been seeing." Wiley's cooking had been taking customers away from Jumbo Gumbos for months. Jumbo Jim could play it down all he wanted, but there was no denying that they were kicking his appetizers.

"I wouldn't say that. Right now, little girl, you are a novelty, but people will get used to you and your substandard food, and then they will forget all about you. Enjoy it while you can. If you would excuse us, we're trying to do some business here. I expect a big crowd today. Some fool invited some sort of cat club to town," Jim said, his smile revealing some stray pieces of brown, greasy chewing tobacco.

Nora stormed back to her car while the men shared a laugh. She was in a bad mood when she arrived at the hotel, and when she informed Wiley of the expected arrival time of the food, he looked like he wanted to cry.

"They're messing with us. You know that, don't you? Jumbo Jim is in cahoots with Moore Foods. I'll bet he paid them a little extra under the table to make our food deliveries late," Wiley said.

"Can we find some chicken elsewhere?" Nora asked.

Caesar held his white cook's hat in his hand. "Miss Nora, I'd be willing to drive to every supermarket in the county to get you some." She was ready to send him on the road, but the only problem was the price they would have to pay for supermarket chicken, and there was no guarantee they could find the right amount for a large crowd. Nora was getting so desperate for chicken that she'd be paying the Colonel himself soon.

"Let me clear it with Marty. Get a figure on how many pounds you're going to need." She turned to Wiley. "How much time do you need to prepare for tomorrow?"

"It needs to be marinated overnight."

"Can you shorten the time any?"

"Yes, but it won't taste as good."

"Fine. I have faith in you. You can make anything taste good." Nora didn't miss the slight shake in her uncle's shoulders.

Deciding to retrieve Izzy's manuscript next, Nora climbed the stairs to the fourth floor, where Jolene was supposed to be putting on the new sheets. Holding her hand on her chest and feeling her heart beating from the impromptu cardio workout of climbing steps, Nora leaned against the door frame of the fourth floor. She hadn't realized how out of shape she was getting. Just as soon as this convention was over, she vowed to herself that she would start some sort of exercise routine every day. This was ridiculous. She wasn't even thirty yet. To her surprise, the door to the elevator was open, revealing the empty shaft and, next to it, the small table that was on its side, resting in the remains of a broken vase, water, and fresh flowers. Pages of Izzy's manuscript were everywhere. A key attached to a keychain from Hickelby's Motor Lodge lay on the carpet.

Nora walked through the scattered debris to the edge of the opening in the elevator. The wood molding around the elevator had a broken edge. Even though the thought of revisiting the elevator shaft frightened her, Nora couldn't help herself and looked down. It was almost too dark to see anything, but her curiosity got the better of her. She walked to the hall supply closet and grabbed one of the flashlights they kept for power outages. Trying to judge the distance down the shaft, she leaned over with one hand balanced on the edge of the doorway opening. Nora aimed her beam of light down the elevator shaft. The elevator car now rested four floors down, so the flashlight beam had a long way to travel. She identified the now-familiar square outline of the car and shivered as she recalled how scary it had been to climb up the elevator shaft.

To her surprise, nestled among the cables was a figure. Nora drew in a breath, and upon recognizing the jumbled heap was a person, she let out a scream. Sprawled on top of the Tunie Hotel elevator was Alan Shaw.

Chapter 6

"So, when was the last time you saw Mr. Shaw?" Tuck asked as they wheeled the unfortunate reporter out of the lobby. Because he had been on top of the elevator car and was in rigamortis, they had to lift him with a basket to the second floor and then carry the dead reporter to the gurney. The strange position of Mr. Shaw's body as it landed in the elevator shaft couldn't be hidden by the body bag. The bulges hung over the side of the rolling cart.

The Meow Meetup convention guests had started trickling in and were lined up at the check-in counter. Thank goodness Marty called in Dominic and Max to cover the check-ins. The crowd was mostly women, and most of them were sporting rolling luggage, a sure sign that climbing the stairs might be a problem. They stole glances as the gurney procession went out the door. Even though the day had only just begun, an overwhelming exhaustion ran through Nora as she searched for the answer to Tuck's question. "I guess when he accosted Evangeline Cartwright in the dining room. After that, if he was around the hotel, I didn't see him."

"Just what exactly happened when he checked in? He said you lost his reservation. Right?"

"Mr. Shaw thought he had a room here, but he didn't. You heard him. He was way out of bounds with the kinds of things he was saying about Evangeline. I thought he was just trying to get an interview with an old lady who writes mysteries," Nora said. Wiley came around the corner with a cup of coffee for his niece. Nora sniffed the brew and figured out there was a little more in it than coffee.

"For your nerves," Wiley whispered before he returned to his post in the kitchen.

"Do you think it was the fall that killed him?" Nora asked after taking a deep sip of the coffee. The added ingredient started to course through her veins, calming her shaky hands.

"We're not totally sure. Probably. We'll know more after the autopsy. Did he make his own reservation, or do you think he was just trying to muscle his way into the hotel?"

"He said his secretary made it for him. We didn't have a booking or a credit card on file. I couldn't give him what I didn't have. He said he was here to cover the convention. Did he have his phone with him? He told me he lost it while traveling here."

"Yes, he had one, but it didn't have any data on it. I think it was one of those cheap ones you can pick up in a hurry."

"Sort of like his bags," Nora said.

"Did you hear anything or see anything unusual last night? Anybody lurking around who shouldn't be?" Tuck asked.

"I didn't see anything. Max was on duty, so you'll have to ask him." Remembering Max was known to catch a few winks on the night shift, Nora had to assume that was when Alan Shaw fell down the elevator shaft.

"Did the victim get his interview?"

"No. At least I don't think he did. It sure didn't sound like it last night. As nice as Evangeline was, she would have given him a few minutes. You called him a victim. Does this mean it is definitely murder?"

"Yes. There were signs of a struggle in the waiting area by the elevator, and pieces of the molding were missing where he tried to anchor himself against his attacker. We're going to need a little more time up there. When will the elevator be fixed?"

"Today, we hope, and do me a favor and keep the murder part to yourself. This could be bad for the Tunie's bottom line right now."

Izzy Franklin came rushing in the door, pushing past the guests waiting in line. "I heard about the murder. Alan Shaw was an awful man. Just about anybody could have pushed him." Once she had paid her respects in that department, Izzy looked Nora in the eye. "Did you find my manuscript?"

"Yes, I did, and we were not even sure that it was murder. It could have been an accident." At least finding the manuscript was one good thing in Nora's day.

"Where is it?"

"Uh, it's in the middle of a crime scene right now."

"What?"

"It was on a table by the elevator on the fourth floor. I'd just found it when I discovered Mr. Shaw in the elevator."

"Excuse me, I know I met you last night, but you seem so familiar to me," Tuck asked, butting in between us.

"Izzy Franklin. I can't believe you don't know me. You reserve those true crime books all the time. Think of me sitting behind a big tan counter. Ring a bell?"

Tuck pressed his lips together and then hit the side of his head with the palm of his hand. "Miss Franklin. The library lady. Yes, you're right. Sometimes it's hard to recognize people when you don't see them in familiar surroundings."

"Yes. I was about to call your office to see if you could charge somebody with mishandling a manuscript." She glared at Nora.

"Izzy. I promise, once the police finish with it, I will personally deliver your manuscript to Miss Cartwright."

"And this time I should believe you?" When she spoke, her glasses slid down her nose, and she glared at Nora over the top of them.

Tuck pulled Nora over, stepping away from Izzy. "Do you have any idea who left that manuscript by the elevator?"

"I don't know for sure. I just assumed ..."

Tuck turned back as a uniformed officer came down the stairs. "I think we're done up there, sir. The fourth-floor guests can check in now. They just need to stay out of the areas where we taped it off."

"Great. I'm sure the hotel wants to make their guests comfortable." He turned to Izzy and said, "Miss Franklin, just how angry were you with our victim last night?"

"He was insulting Evangeline Cartwright. She's the best writer in the country, and she certainly didn't deserve to be spoken to in that way. I don't know why the hotel didn't just get rid of him sooner. They certainly seem to get rid of other things pretty easily."

Nora winced at the obvious criticism of her handling of the manuscript.

Tuck continued. "And would you protect your writing hero enough to say, push someone down the elevator shaft?"

Nora gave him a withering glance. "But we know it was an accident..."

Izzy's eyes widened. She didn't look strong enough to push Alan Shaw's bulk anywhere. Tuck Watson's query seemed ludicrous.

Izzy crossed her arms and raised her chin. "If you plan to ask me questions like that, I'll have to request there be a lawyer present."

"Of course." Tuck nodded respectfully.

Izzy turned back to Nora and pointed a finger in her face. "I'll be back in a few hours." Izzy leaned over, bringing her face uncomfortably close to Nora's. "Miss Cartwright had better be looking through that manuscript by then."

"Of course," Nora said, parroting Tuck. Nora found herself holding back a sneeze. As much as Nora tried to control it, she let out a tremendous noise.

"God bless you," Tuck said, reaching for a hankie in his pocket.

A woman in a baggy animal-print sweatshirt covered in cat hair who was checking in gave Nora a look. "You should be sneezing into the crook of your arm, you know."

"I'm sorry. I didn't know I was going to sneeze. I thought I'd stopped it."

"Obviously," the woman said, pulling out a tiny bottle of hand sanitizer.

Tuck looked around the lobby. The Tunie was suddenly very busy as the undercurrent of female voices began filling the room. "I'd better get upstairs and make sure the crime scene crew did everything they were supposed to." He drew Nora closer and was about to kiss her when, once again, she sneezed.

"Drawing on my detective skills, I need to ask you a question. Are you allergic to cats?" he asked.

"Yes," Nora groaned.

"Oh my, nothing like a hotel full of guests covered in cat dander," he said, a smile in his eyes.

A man dressed in a gray uniform came into the lobby and made his way through the crowd.

"Excuse me. I've come to work on the elevator."

Nora sure hoped cleaning off the top of the elevator car was part of the service. She would need to check petty cash for a tip. A big tip.

Chapter 7

At noon, the guests were almost all checked in, eating lunch, and settling down for a cat nap. The crime scene was cleared, and the elevator was running. Even though none of the guests had been allowed to bring their beloved pets, the hotel felt like it was overrun with cats in the form of cat purses, t-shirts, shoes, and jackets. Everything was working out. Marty had even reported that the swelling was going down on her ankle.

"How did you know I forgot to pack a lunch?" Nora said as Tatty Tovar walked in, waving a bag of fast food.

Tatty grinned. "Let's just say that after getting to know you, I was pretty sure you would only be thinking of this hotel. Besides, I wanted to see all the doings at the Tunie."

"Not that exciting, if you don't count Mr. Shaw's death."

"Another reason I'm here. I heard about it already from Mrs. Cantrell across the street, who heard it when she was shopping at the Texas Star Market. How are you doing? It looks like you sailed through it somehow."

"I know, right? He was a terrible little man, but he didn't deserve to die like he did. Tuck is on the case, though." Nora opened her bag, and then, as a sneeze overtook her, she shut it again.

Tatty pulled a tissue from the tissue box on the counter and then handed it to Nora. "The cat dander is thick around here. People carry it on their clothes. You're going to have to clean everywhere after they leave."

"I know. I know. I'm figuring out why no one else would take this group. Now that we can put this on our convention resume, we won't be offering our facility to them next year."

"If you can keep the rooms rented when all your future guests start sneezing."

"It's not that bad. The real problem right now is Wiley and the restaurant. Our supplier was supposed to deliver a big order of chicken for the keynote dinner tonight." Nora checked her watch. "It was supposed to be here about five minutes ago."

"Where does he get his chicken?"

"Moore Foods, and even though he thinks he put the order in, they say they never received it."

"That's strange."

"The thing is, Jumbo Gumbo seems to be getting their shipments with no problems. You know, when I started working here, I thought something like booking a convention was easy. We pulled off an incredible party to celebrate the Tunie, but I had to be crazy thinking I could handle something like this. I haven't even studied hospitality."

"You can do that?"

"Sure, it's a major in college. They offer it down at the University of Houston."

"So, what? You don't have a degree in hotel management, but you do have a degree. You have all the smarts you need, Nora. Ed and I don't have any degrees, and we're doing just fine. Frankly, I don't think you need one. You've already turned the Tunie completely around. Before you came, Marty was drowning in this place."

Nora sighed, feeling the weight of the world on her shoulders. "I suppose you're right."

Tatty looked around the lobby. "Is it okay if we eat our hamburgers right here?"

"As long as I don't have anybody checking in, I don't think there's a problem."

Wiley came out of the kitchen with an expectant look on his face. "Have you heard anything?"

"Not yet. Don't you need to be in the kitchen?"

"No. What I need is forty pounds of chicken. How am I supposed to serve marinated chicken if I can't marinate it?"

Nora leaned her elbows on the desk, her fingers around her hamburger. "I don't know. What is the fastest thing you can do with chicken?"

Wiley shrugged with a sour look on his face. "Fry it, I guess, but anybody can do that."

"Then be ready to make that, but better."

"I thought you said you straightened this out. I knew Jumbo Jim would slow us down."

"Go back to the kitchen, Uncle Wiley. I'll give them another call." He started to open his mouth, but Nora stopped him. "Go!"

Wiley stomped off to the dining room.

Tatty's eyes slid to a squint along with a smile. "You told him. You know everybody in town is talking about Wiley's food here."

"Did I tell you that he studied at culinary school?"

Tatty was in the middle of a bite of her hamburger when she looked up in surprise. "No way. You mean we have a chef among us, and we never knew it?"

"Yes, but his history with alcohol always messed up his chances of advancement."

"How is he doing now?"

"Pretty good. Uncle Wiley tells me he's going to AA meetings. If anything is going to test his sobriety, it will be all these cat ladies."

"You have a very interesting family. By the way, how is that newfound brother of yours?" Tatty asked. The same time Nora found out that Lucy was her half sister, she found out that Corey Brockwell, the town's richest and most spoiled son, was her half brother.

"I guess Lucy paid a visit to Corey before she left for New York to ask where our quarterly earnings were from Brockwell Industries."

"And what did he tell her?"

"Not a lot. I think he's holding back on us. He's strangely calm these days. Maybe he's taken up yoga or something. I'm guessing he has no money to give us because he's already spent it. He's probably keeping a low profile to hide from the loan sharks he owes money to."

Since Adam Brockwell's death, all his property had been sold off, and the profit was to be divided by his three children. It was Corey's job to report back to his sisters on a quarterly basis with profits and losses. If it came to be that Corey was mishandling the business, then Nora and Lucy would step in.

"I heard he went on a terrible bender after the house sold," Tatty said. For Corey Brockwell, a terrible bender meant gambling and lots of it. "I'll bet he's gambled away all of his inheritance."

"Well, if we don't get something from Corey soon, we're going to have to call Harvey, our father's lawyer."

Tatty looked at her watch. "I left Ed planting flowers on the walk. It's best not to let him alone for too long. He tends to take a nap." She looked around the empty lobby. "You know, and I'm not being critical here, but it seems if you have a big convention crowd, I would expect to see more people."

"The opening cocktail party is at four in the banquet room."

Tatty smiled and put her nose up in the air. "A cocktail party in the banquet room, aren't we fancy?"

"That's cat fanciers to you."

As Tatty picked up her purse, a guest came in the door. The middle-aged woman struggled to balance her bags, and Tatty, always helpful, extended her hands.

"Can I help carry something?" Tatty asked before Nora could.

The woman nodded at her gratefully. "If you would grab my book bag, that would be great. Thank you so much, dear."

"No problem," Tatty responded. She gently took a fabric tote full of hardback books written by Evangeline Cartwright and placed it in front of Nora at the counter.

Nora smiled her best hospitality smile and said, "Welcome to the Tunie. I take it you're here for the Meow Meetup." As she finished her sentence, a giant sneeze escaped. She didn't see any cat hair on this woman, but her eyes began to water, and the inside of her nose tickled.

"I'll see you back at the B&B, and I'll make sure Ed puts a fresh box of tissues in your room," Tatty said.

"What would I do without you?" Nora answered after her, the red circles under her eyes now standing out against the red of her hair. After checking in her latest guest, Nora remembered her promise to Wiley and dialed the number for Moore's Food. At her insistence, she was put through to a manager.

"You say you checked with Beth this morning?"

The woman on the other end sounded confused to Nora. That in itself was baffling. It was like the order had never been placed. "Yes, and she promised our chicken would be delivered by noon. We are still waiting for it, and we have a hotel full of guests expecting to eat."

"Oh, my. Honestly, I'm new here, but let me just look."

There was the sound of papers shuffling on the other end, and then the woman returned to the phone. "You're not going to believe this, but I just found the paperwork for your order underneath another. I'll have the truck loaded in the next ten minutes. You should have your chicken soon."

Nora's whole mood lightened. Finally, someone was doing their job over there. "That's wonderful. Thank you. What is your name?"

"Val. I just signed on as office manager over here, and frankly, I think I was hired because this kind of thing keeps happening. If it's okay with you, I'm going to ride along with the driver just to make sure you get your chicken, and please accept my apologies."

"Thank you so much, Val."

"Thank you for putting up with this malarkey. The Tunie should be treated with respect. It's a town landmark for goodness' sake."

Feeling good about her call with Moore Foods, Nora stepped away from the front desk and found Wiley in the kitchen. He was pulling out giant bags of flour, causing a haze of white powder to float everywhere. This wouldn't be a gluten-free night, for sure. "Hey Wiley, you should have your chicken in the next hour. Check to see if you have everything you need to get to work."

Wiley grumbled, "Professionally trained chef, and I'm frying up a mess of chicken."

Chapter 8

When Nora returned, a couple of guests were lined up to check in. Marty leaned over the desk, balancing precariously on one foot. "What are you doing here?" Nora asked.

"I was checking the webcam of the lobby on my phone and saw there were some new guests needing to be checked in. I thought for sure I could take care of at least one guest." Marty had put the webcam in months ago, thinking it would be a terrific way for her to watch the front desk if she didn't have somebody to cover it. Nora didn't expect it to become a reason for Marty to hobble down from her apartment. Marty flashed an ankle that was now turning a serious shade of purple. "Look. The swelling is going down." The woman at the counter cringed.

"Excuse her, ma'am," Nora said to the woman at the front of the line. "She just wanted to make sure you were being taken care of, and we hope you enjoy the convention." Nora turned back to Marty. "You should be upstairs resting. I don't care who you see on that webcam. We have it under control."

"I know. It's just so hard to be upstairs while all of this is going on down here. On top of everything else, after I checked in one guest, the software stopped working. I can't believe it. I keep trying to put in the name, but the software freezes." Marty furiously tapped on the computer as if the pressure she put on the tiny plastic keys would make a difference. "Do you have any idea what might be going on?"

Nora looked at the computer screen as it flashed a warning box she had never seen before. She reached to the side of the computer and flipped it off.

"Oh, my God, what are you doing?" Marty's skin took on an even paler shade.

"You said you wanted me to fix it. Sometimes the best thing you can do for a computer is give it a time out."

"This is not a misbehaving child."

"Oh, yes, it is." Nora flipped the switch again, and the computer began rebooting. Marty's exhaustion was evident as she leaned on one elbow. The computer beeped, and the home screen began to come up.

"There you go. Up and running." As Nora finished her sentence, a sneeze engulfed her. These allergies were going to be the death of her. The woman with the cell phone ended up being in the direct line of fire.

She stepped back again, bumping into someone behind her. "Really." Her voice was drawn out, showing great disdain.

"I'm so sorry. Did I get you?" The woman's eyes rolled in answer to Nora's question. Nora tried to make light of the situation. "Who knew it? Funny thing, actually. I'm allergic to cats, and it seems, people who live with cats." Nora gave a quick smile as the computer continued to warm up and then turned Marty in the direction of the elevators. "I'll take care of this. You go back upstairs." She looked at the guest who had put away her cell phone and was now tapping her leopard-skin Keds against the red lobby carpet.

Nora motioned her forward and said, "I'll check you in now."

"It's about time," the guest snapped.

As Marty released her hold on the desk, she said to Nora, "You're a godsend; did you know that? Thanks for being here. Maybe I'll just take a nap. It is starting to ache a little."

"Just remember, we can handle this. We are all trained to do this. We just have to figure out how to do it for more people."

"You're right. I was being silly. I leave the hotel in your capable hands," Marty said as she made her way to the stairway door.

The booking software came up refreshed and ready to work. "Thank God for that," Nora whispered to herself, revealing that she had been unsure if her quick fix would've worked. She checked in the guest with great efficiency, wanting to get the woman and her attitude away from the check-in desk.

Evangeline Cartwright came into the lobby. Upon seeing the police, she lowered her chin to her chest. "What happened? I'm afraid I slept like a baby last night."

This was amazing because an altercation with Alan Shaw resulting in his falling down the elevator, not to mention the entire crime scene investigation, had occurred right outside her door. "You didn't hear anything?"

"No. It's strange because, usually, I have trouble sleeping when I'm traveling. I guess the Tunie must feel like home to me. What happened?"

Nora continued checking in the next customer while carrying on her conversation with Evangeline. "The reporter who was badgering you at dinner—you didn't happen to know him, did you?"

"I never laid eyes on him until last night. He certainly was a disagreeable little man."

"That disagreeable little man was found dead today," Nora told her. The guest, who had been putting away her credit card, nearly dropped her entire bag on the carpet.

"You're on the third floor," Nora said, handing her a room key. "We hope you enjoy your stay at the Tunie." The lady was reluctant to leave, but gave Nora a quick smile and headed for the elevator. Nora turned back to Evangeline in a conspiratorial fashion.

Evangeline gulped. "Okay. What happened?"

Not wanting to give any more guests a chance to hear crime details, Nora answered her in a soft voice. News of a death could spread through a crowd like wildfire, and the Tunie would never see another convention booking again. She had already probably set the wheels in motion by talking in front of the last guest. She would have to be more careful from here on out. It could be unbelievably bad for their bottom line, especially if they decided that the poor maintenance of the elevator was at fault. "He sort of fell down the elevator shaft." As warm and lovely as Evangeline was to be around, she just couldn't tell her it was being looked at as murder.

"I see. That would explain the police being on my floor. That's terrible. Just terrible."

"I can't believe you didn't hear it." Nora looked up at the glass lobby door to see a new set of guests get out of a minivan. Upon entering, they formed a line at the front desk. One woman looked Evangeline's way and, after rustling in her purse, stepped over with a pristine paperback copy of a novel.

The woman held out the book under Evangeline's nose. "Would you sign this for me?"

"Certainly, do you have a pen?"

The hotel guest gave Evangeline a brown cat-paw-covered pen. Max strolled into the lobby wearing a three-piece suit complete with a vest. Nora noticed his hair had taken on a bit more of a brown tint. The vest was blue and white striped, reminding Nora of an outfit that might be worn by a member of a barbershop quartet. They exchanged a glance.

"Is Marty upstairs?" he said, his eyes darting around the lobby. The phone rang immediately.

"Yes. She came down a minute ago when she saw a customer on her lobby webcam."

"And you let her?"

"I couldn't stop her." The phone continued ringing, and Nora picked it up. "Front desk."

"Tell Max I appreciate him dressing up for the convention, but why doesn't he take off that coat and vest? Our guests will start asking him if his ice cream truck is outside."

"Hold on, I'll put you on speaker, and you can tell him yourself." Nora punched the button on the phone and went back to checking in the guests.

Marty's voice came out of the phone speaker. "Max? A little overdressed for the Tunie don't you think?"

"Just showing a little professionalism, my dear. I'm thinking maybe we need a dress code for behind the desk." Max straightened his tie and pulled down the seat of his jacket.

"If you say so," Marty said, hanging up.

"I didn't know men even wore three-piece suits anymore," Nora said, trying to think of the last time she saw a man in a vest all the while running a credit card.

Max puffed out his chest. "I'm trying to look like Tom Selleck in *Blue Bloods*."

Nora nodded but had a tough time seeing any sort of resemblance to the television actor.

Max quietly looked her way and dipped his chin. "Not working?"

Nora shrugged. She couldn't hurt this sweet bear of a man, so as her mother would have told her, if you can't say something nice... Without warning, a thunderous sneeze came out of her. The woman who was trying to check in flinched at the oncoming nasal avalanche.

Max handed her a tissue. "God bless you, Nora. I think I'll get a soda, and then I'll head upstairs to check on Marty. You can handle it for a few minutes, right? I, uh, brought her something." Max ambled over to the snack alcove and started reaching for his normal soft drink, but then switched at the last moment to bottled water. He was really making some changes.

"Sure. Take your time," Nora said.

After Evangeline finished signing the book, she turned back to Nora and raised her hand, speaking out of earshot of the guests in a conspiratorial fashion. "I'm allergic to the little beasts myself." Surprised by Evangeline's frank confession, Nora was relieved her sneezing wasn't misinterpreted as someone who hated cats. Evangeline patted Nora on the shoulder. "Some breeds of cats cause people to sneeze. Did you know cats can put humans in the hospital with upper respiratory problems?"

"I had no idea how contagious I was until this convention."

"I've been to many of these conventions, and I have to tell you, being in your quaint hotel has been a very comfortable thing for me. No wonder I slept through a police investigation. You have provided more than hospitality here, but a feeling of home."

"Thank you. I really appreciate that, and we are honored to serve you," Nora said.

Tuck stepped into the lobby, holding on to the manuscript encased in a transparent plastic bag. The ripped mailing envelope was now stained with fingerprint dust.

"Izzy's manuscript! I can't thank you enough." Nora placed a kiss on Tuck's cheek.

"If that's my payment, no, you can't." Tuck grinned and then stepped over to the coffee alcove for a honeybun. "We picked up the loose pages and returned them to the envelope, but it's a mess. By the way, if you are going to be having crime scenes here at the hotel, you'll need to be stocking a lot more donuts over here. I'll put a dollar in the till for the bun."

"I know you will," Nora said as she began to fan Max with a folder. "And this *accident* scene will be our last. Don't expect a return engagement."

"Would your find have anything to do with the hopeful writer I met last night, or is this *your* manuscript?" Evangeline said, eyeing the plastic bag.

"Nope. Not mine. I'm more of a true crime guy myself. Your hopeful writer wanted us to deliver this to you, but we need to check for prints on all three hundred pages inside."

Evangeline smiled wistfully. "All right, then. I'm sure the writer wanted that story to have a thorough going-over, but maybe this was not what she had in mind."

A deep, cloying smell of perfume reached Nora's nose before a woman in sleek black leggings and a white frilly halter top stepped into the lobby. She pulled off her oversized sunglasses to reveal stunning hazel eyes rimmed in gold. They had been artfully lined with black eyeliner tipping up in the corners, making her resemble a cat. Tuck turned around, taking in the sexy cat lady slinking toward the check-in line.

His gaze didn't leave the new guest. "I can see you're getting busy. I should get going. It was nice meeting you, Miss Cartwright, and for your sake, I hope the rest of your stay is uneventful."

As Tuck spoke, the darkly beautiful woman turned, leaving her place in line. She strolled over to the group and extended a hand to Evangeline. "Hello, Miss Cartwright. What an honor to meet you. I'm Sasha LeClaire, and I would love to get an interview for my website, Cat Aficionado. I am not much of a mystery reader myself. I prefer literary fiction, but many of my readers seem to have a liking for your work. It could be fun." Sasha LeClaire's compliment was the highest form of passive aggression, but Evangeline did not seem to be concerned by it.

"Oh, yes. I'm familiar with your website. If we can work you in, I'd be glad to speak with you."

"Perrrfect," Sasha said, fluttering her eyelashes in Tuck's direction. Her gaze held him for a moment, and then she moved back to Evangeline. The color rose to his cheeks. "It is always so good for me to diversify on my website. I tend to focus more on cat health, but don't you just love a delightful story about cats?"

Her almond-shaped eyes zeroed back in on Tuck, who gulped and then repeated. "I'm more of a true crime guy myself."

Chapter 9

An hour later, most of the guests had gone to their rooms, but a few still trickled in.

"Excuse me," a woman with tightly curled blond hair stood in front of the check-in desk. Where others had climbed off the van from the airport with various t-shirts and sweatshirts sporting pictures of cats, she wore a suit jacket with a flowing silk blouse underneath and a well-fitted skirt. She looked comfortable in her matching heels, indicating she was a woman who wore dress shoes most of the time.

"Yes, how can I help you?" Nora answered.

"I'm Camille Martin-Ortega, the organizer of the Meow Meetup. I had a few concerns I needed to discuss with the owner. Can you get him on the phone for me?"

"I can help you," Nora assured her.

"I appreciate your can-do spirit, but just get your boss on the phone."

"I am the boss. I'm one of the owners of the Tunie." The convention organizer paled, but then went on as if her sexist slight was of no importance.

"I see. You certainly could have said something. I find it inconsiderate of you to make me feel foolish."

"My apologies. You had some concerns?"

"Yes. When we booked this hotel for our convention, the girl on the phone promised us that this was a top-quality establishment. Not everyone was in tune with our needs, so we settled on a venue that was slightly out of the way. We are one of the smaller cat gatherings in the United States, but we hope to grow in the future. Since checking in, there has been a man killed due to an inoperative elevator, and now we are finding that this is only a one-star hotel. Frankly, the whole thing reeks of false advertising."

"I can assure you the one-star rating is a mistake." Nora knew it was wrong to think ill of the dead, but Alan Shaw was responsible for this.

"Time to wake up and smell the litter box, my dear," the convention organizer stated. "That many people leaving a one-star rating is no mistake. Your guests have spoken, and clearly this hotel has failed."

"If I could just explain..."

Camille Martin-Ortega raised a palm to the air. "Considering this undisclosed information and the health hazards my association members have faced at the Tunie, I am demanding a discount. I believe 50 percent would be a proper reimbursement." Her tightly held curls bobbed just a bit as she stood firm with her chin raised in the air.

"I'll need to speak to my partner about your concern, Miss Ortega."

"Martin-Ortega," she corrected.

Whatever, Nora thought.

After the pushy organizer of the Meow Meetup left, Nora thought of Marty and the trust she had placed in her. Now that they had booked this convention, the hotel had a better chance of booking other gatherings. Nora had taken it upon herself to start contacting state organizations to see if the Tunie was a good fit. To prepare for the Meow Meetup, Marty and Nora had invested in many extras that had eaten up the savings they had worked so hard to collect. If they had to cut the cost of the convention guests' room fee in half, they would lose money. Nora pulled herself together and put on a smile as a group of ladies came from the dining room. "I hope you enjoyed your lunch, ladies," Nora said.

"It was just incredible food!"

"I'll be sure and tell the cook. Thank you so much for your compliments."

"It was quite a surprise," one woman said. "When we were told we were coming to a small town in Texas, the last thing we thought we were going to get would be decent food. I'm going to remember this place."

"Those are wonderful words to hear, ladies. I hope you enjoy your afternoon." It was slowing down in the lobby, and Nora was about to check Rate Your Hotel to make sure no more reviews had popped up. After hearing the glowing words of the convention guests, she would hate for that last batch of satisfied customers to read the lies Alan Shaw had left. Before Nora could pull up the website, Bert Hickelby of Hickelby's Motor Lodge came into the lobby with two cheap leatherette bags that Nora immediately recognized. He threw them on the floor. "Here ya'go." After dropping the bags, he threw both hands up in the air in finality.

Nora eyed the luggage. "What am I supposed to do with these bags?"

"Whatever you want to. You dumped this guy on me, and then you killed him in that contraption you call an elevator *before* he paid his bill."

"Didn't you take a credit card?"

"Hickelby's Motor Lodge deals on a cash-only basis."

Nora well understood why Hickelby operated on cash instead of credit. The Motor Lodge was a favorite of cheating spouses in the area. No paper trails.

"I believe I'm entitled to the cost of his room rent for one night. He disappeared, and I was unable to rent the room to anyone else. I missed out on a night's rent, and when it comes to money, it is no joking matter over at Hickelby's. You may be running a big mega-hotel here, but over at Hickelby's, we are still a small-time family enterprise. I'll wait while you write me a check."

Bert Hickelby stood, tapping his toe, waiting for Nora's response. His rabbit-like eyes darted back and forth. He was playing a game with her. Hotels had to absorb costs from no-show guests every day. If he took a loss on a guest, that was his problem, not the Tunie's. Nora gave him a slow, steady look, making him think she was considering his demand.

"Do you know what, Bert? I think you're just going to have to eat the cost of one night's rent on your brother-in-law's old room."

His eyes widened, and his bottom lip trembled a bit. "Do you know how much money that is?"

"Forty dollars?" Nora guessed.

He put a hand to his throat in mock terror. "I am insulted! We raised the rates to forty-six ninety-nine last April. We wanted to discourage the riff-raff. If you want to round it up to an even fifty, I won't complain."

"You are too kind."

He brightened up at Nora's words, thinking he had just made a deal. Nora continued. "What am I supposed to do with these bags?"

"I guess you should call wherever this dude worked and ask where to send them. I, myself, Bert Hickelby, refuse to put up with the cost of shipping some loser dead guy's luggage. I heard that Yankee accent. That should've been my first clue that something like this would happen. Postage up North is way out of my budget."

"Fine. I'll make you a deal."

Bert Hickelby smacked his lips. "I knew you had a head for business, little lady."

"You eat the cost of the room, and I'll take care of Alan Shaw's luggage." Nora crossed her arms, her feet firm on the ground. She wasn't budging, and it didn't take long for Bert Hickelby to see that.

"You can't be serious. It was because you lost his reservation that he was dumped on our fine establishment. No. This will not do."

"Fine. No deal at all, and you take the luggage back. It was not nice doing business with you." Nora gave a forced smile and then turned her back on him, straightening the papers on the copy machine.

Bert Hickelby was getting nowhere fast. "Okay. Okay fine. Have it your way. We'll forget about the cost of the room, and you get this guy's bags off my hands. I still don't like it, but because I'm a man of compromise, you have a deal." He reached down and fingered the plastic vinyl of the bags. "These are pretty nice bags here. I'm not quite sure if this was fair."

Nora came around the desk to pick up the bags, stopped, and put both hands on Bert's shoulders. She turned him toward the door and gave him a slight push. "Don't worry. I won't be cashing in on the bags. Pleather doesn't bring the dollar it used to," she called after him as he walked out.

Chapter 10

Nora pulled Alan Shaw's luggage behind the desk. She would have to notify Tuck. He would need them for his investigation. She had a few minutes to look, so she hoisted one of the bags on the counter. She unzipped it and looked inside. Nothing was out of order here. There were several changes of clothes, underwear that had seen better days, and a copy of the cat magazine where he said he worked.

Maybe that would be where she could start to find his mailing address. As she searched, there wasn't anything in the bag that left a trail of clues about his assignment to interview Evangeline Cartwright. There wasn't a notebook or anything else that seemed to have anything to do with the mystery writer.

Alan Shaw had been an obnoxious little man, and instead of trying to find one person he made angry, Nora had to assume the police were overwhelmed with weeding through scores of people. The last time she saw the tenacious reporter alive, he had been spewing hatred toward Evangeline and Doug. Did Mr. Shaw have a crush on Evangeline? He had acted like seeing her and Doug together was a terrible thing. Was that because he was a jealous admirer? Had he been like Izzy, just in male form? Evangeline might write a heck of a mystery, but the idea of her having two men fighting over her at the age of sixty-five was pretty out there. She looked like somebody's grandmother.

There was something about that evening before that struck her as out of place. It was like when Nora methodically straightened the chairs in the dining room during her evening shift. Each one had to be centered on the square of the table. She knew it was part of her history as a personal organizer, but there was a sense of peace in seeing everything in its place. Thinking back on the scene with Izzy and Alan interrupting Evangeline's dinner, something was not aligned correctly.

A truck horn beeped from the alley. After stowing the luggage, she speed walked to the service entrance, hoping it was Moore Foods. Wiley joined her, matching his pace to hers. A pleasantly plump woman jumped down from the passenger side of the truck cab. "Are you Nora?"

"I sure am. Are you Val?"

"Guilty." When she smiled, little dimples played in the corners of her cheeks. Nora instantly liked her.

Wiley bowed to her politely in two jerky motions and then ran to the back of the truck, his excitement taking over his ability to speak.

"That was our chef. He's very glad to see you."

Val shook her head. "I'm so sorry about what happened to you." She leaned closer and spoke in a whisper. "You were right. Your driver here has been up to something. He wasn't very happy when I told him I wanted to ride along for this little run."

Nora nodded in agreement. "If I had to guess, I would say he's getting a little cash under the table from Jumbo Gumbos to slow our deliveries."

Val edged closer, her eyes widening in astonishment. "Do you have any proof?"

"Not a bit. It's just a feeling," Nora answered. There was probably almost no way to prove it. Like Hickelby's, she was sure Jumbo Jim worked on a cash basis.

"Don't worry about it. If he's getting his palm greased, I'll catch him." Val straightened up as the driver came around the corner with several boxes on a dolly.

"Right through here, in case you've forgotten after all this time," Wiley said as he directed the man to the kitchen, his thin frame all business now.

Val nodded and said, "Would you mind if I came inside? I haven't been to the Tunie in years."

Nora took on the role of hostess. "Of course. Let me show you around. We've made some improvements."

Val smiled once again, displaying her dimples. "Oh, you don't need to show me around. I know where everything is. I used to work here, you know."

"You did?"

"Sure. Mr. Tunie hired me to wait tables in the dining room. I also doubled for missing maids on occasion. It's not my favorite job, to be sure. People are pigs." Val slowed her step and gazed at the wall of mementos. "I loved this place. It was a part of my childhood, I guess. I was sorry to see Mr. Tunie sell it."

She fingered the edge of the couches and then peeked into the dining room. She turned abruptly. "Is the ballroom still there?" The ballroom, as she put it, had now turned into a banquet and conference room. Nora and Marty had booked meetings and even classes. Occasionally, though, there was still dancing attached to an event. The Tunie was becoming especially popular with weddings.

"That's the thing about this place. Everyone has a history here." Val opened the doors to the room where Evangeline Cartwright would deliver her keynote speech in a few hours. "Beautiful. It feels like coming home."

The phone rang from behind the desk. Nora excused herself and quickly answered, "Front desk."

"Val? Do I see Val in my lobby?" Marty had been watching them from her webcam again.

"Yes. Do you know her? She came over with the delivery from Moore Foods. Did you want to speak with her?" Nora inquired.

"I sure did. That girl still owes me five bucks and a Snickers bar." Nora turned to Val. "It's for you."

"Me? Work usually calls me on my cell phone. I wonder if the ringer is off." Val said.

"It's not work. It's Marty Reynolds."

"Marty!" Val ran to the offered phone. "Marty? Is it really you? Where are you?"

Nora watched as Val and Marty began to relive old times over the phone. It seemed that when Val worked at the Tunie, so did Marty. As Nora listened, she also picked up on the fact that Val had just moved back to Piney Woods with her children after a divorce. Val hung up and turned to Nora. "What a wonderful surprise! I can't believe she owns the place," Val said, not realizing that Nora also had a part of the Tunie.

"So, you just moved back to town with your children? I couldn't help overhearing." Normally she would have stepped away and given a guest privacy when they were on the phone, but something had held her there.

"Sure did. Two rascally boys. What I don't have any more is a rascally husband. I have custody of the kids for the school year. He gets them in the summer. When I decided to move, there was just one place I wanted to go."

"Piney Woods?"

"You bet. Now I find out my new job is to deliver food to the Tunie. It couldn't get any better than that."

Nora agreed, "You have no idea how happy I am to hear it."

"Yeah, well, those late deliveries you've been having have just become a thing of the past."

"Thanks to you, our problem seems to be solved. This convention started out roughly, but now I think the worst part might be over."

"Only because you hopped on it. What would Marty do without her little helper?" Val remarked.

Nora smiled and dug her toes into the carpet. She knew she should correct Val at this point, but she didn't. She would tell her eventually. She was just glad her presence had put a spark back into Marty.

Chapter 11

While Val got the shipment situated, she spoke of some of the shenanigans she had been uncovering at Moore Foods. She wasn't happy there, and when Nora was deep in discussion with Wiley and Cesar about substitutions, she excused herself. When Nora returned to the front desk, Dominic Fazio was holding up an application. The Tunie Hotel had been written up several times for possible hauntings, and when Nora and Marty put an ad in the paper for a clerk, Dominic jumped at the chance. At forty years old, he remained unmarried, with a long history of serial dating. He told Max one night that he was happy being a perpetual bachelor. The Tunie Hotel, though, did offer him a place to conduct his paranormal investigations. Nora still wasn't sure if this was a good idea or not. If he found a ghost, they might get extra bookings from ghost hunter types, but on the flip side, people might avoid a "haunted hotel." Either way, he was a pretty good employee.

"You're not going to believe this. Somebody actually applied to work here. Wonders never cease."

Nora walked forward and started reading through the neatly lettered answers on the form. An application from someone off the street was an oddity because when Nora came to work for the Tunie Hotel, it was in such a state of disrepair that no one in town even knew the place was open. Back then, no one wanted to hitch their wagon to the failing hotel with the possibility of not having a job the next week.

Not only was it a surprise to get the application, but it was a bit of a shock. It was from the hotel restaurant's newfound friend at Moore Foods.

Nora instantly liked Val, and after getting so much avoidance and subterfuge from their wholesale food supplier, it was wonderful to find someone who was there for the in-house restaurant. She hadn't expected that Val would apply for work at the hotel. As Nora glanced at the application, a tiny amount of anxiety rose in her chest. Val had attended the hotel and restaurant school at the University of Houston. Not only that, but she had worked at a couple of the big hotels in downtown Dallas. With all the problems that were occurring during this convention, would Val have let so many catastrophes explode at the same time? Would there have been so many things beyond Val's control? After looking at Val's track record and her references, Nora highly doubted it.

"So, what should we do with it? Should I get her on the horn so she can come back for an interview?" Dominic asked.

"Let me hold on to this so that I can show it to Marty later," Nora answered. Whether she showed it to her was more of a question than a statement in Nora's mind. What would it be like to work with two people who were so instantly close to each other again? Nora welcomed the idea of hiring somebody competent, but the insecurity that she was feeling overwhelmed her good judgment. She was ashamed that the thought of hiding the application was bouncing around in her head.

"You know what? I might lose it. I'll just stick it in the drawer." Nora put the application under the stack of empty ones.

"Don't you want to put that on the top?" Dominic asked.

"Uh," Nora said, tapping the pile of paper. "We need to keep the personal information on our applications out of the public eye."

Dominic couldn't hide his confusion but took Nora's word. "Sure. Confidentiality. I would hate for someone to accidentally see her address or something. Aye?"

"It would be awful." Nora was thankful that he accepted her explanation. It might be just what they needed—to have someone with hotel management education on their staff. Marty hadn't had any kind of training, but she carried on managing the hotel without it. It wasn't like that in the beginning. Marty broke down more than once and confessed she felt like she made a giant mistake scooping up the Tunie at a bargain price. She feared she would lose everything she had ever worked for, and now Nora worried that sinking her inheritance into this place might have been her mistake.

"And what do we do with this guy's luggage?" Dominic pointed to the two abandoned bags underneath the check-in desk. Alan Shaw's luggage remained where Nora had dropped it.

"I forgot about those. I'll grab them." Nora dragged the bags into the business office, situated just off the lobby. She had also forgotten to call Tuck but wanted to go through the bags one more time. She was sure he was the source of the one-star ratings on Rate My Hotel. After that, she needed to deal with Camille Martin-Ortega. She was starting to feel guilty for asking Marty to go out on a limb with this thing. Now here they were amid the convention with a murder investigation and a distinct possibility that the hotel would be further in the red after so much work, money, and time invested.

Nora stowed the bags in the office. Looking out to the lobby to make sure no one needed her, she quietly closed the door. Along with Alan Shaw's luggage was a small laptop computer that she had seen him carry on the first day. Nora started the computer up but found it was password-protected. The wallpaper on his laptop screen was a scene from the movie *All the President's Men*, showing Woodward and Bernstein, the investigative reporters who broke the story on the Watergate scandal back in the seventies. She tried several passwords, but time after time, a little box popped up with a message telling her it was invalid. Tuck put his head in the door, causing her to jump. She quickly closed the laptop. She smiled. Having time alone with Tuck in the middle of the day was unexpected.

"Am I interrupting something?" He came closer, slipping his hand around her waist. Nora was relieved that he didn't seem to have picked up on what she was doing. Maybe he thought it was her laptop.

"No. Just work."

He glanced at the desk. "What have you got there? Did you get a new laptop?" One thing about having a cop for her boyfriend was that he was always observant. He knew what Nora's laptop looked like, and this was not it. Considering the alternative first, Nora decided to tell the truth. "Bert Hickelby dropped off Alan Shaw's luggage for me to ship back to his next of kin this morning. I was about to call you."

He drew back. "Wasn't his luggage here?"

"No. He wasn't staying at our hotel. He was staying at Hickelby's Motor Lodge. Remember, I told you. He thought he had made a reservation, but it wasn't in our system. He blamed it on us, but we had no record of a reservation."

"And these are his bags?" Tuck now surveyed the bags in a proprietary manner. "I can't believe my guys missed that."

"Bert Hickelby couldn't wait to get rid of them. He didn't want to pay the cost of shipping these things to his family."

Tuck pulled out his cell phone and began a call. "Hey, did you guys get any luggage for Alan Shaw?" Tuck's face began to register annoyance. Clearly, they had not tracked down Shaw's luggage. "The reason I'm asking is that I have it right here in front of me. It was at Hickelby's Motor Lodge, and you guys missed this. I'm bringing it over right now." Tuck ended the conversation and returned to Nora. "Good news. You don't have to deal with trying to ship these bags off to Mr. Shaw's family."

Nora was happy to cooperate with the police, especially this policeman, but if she had to relinquish the bags, that would mean that she would have a tough time proving that Alan Shaw was the one-star guest.

"Something wrong?" Tuck asked.

"No. Well, yes. We have been receiving some very bad ratings online, and I was trying to figure out if Mr. Shaw might have left the reviews. Is there any way I could keep them another day?"

"No. These bags are police evidence."

Nora reached out and slipped her fingers under Tuck's collar as she spoke. "Come on. What harm would it do?"

"None, I guess, but it is not police policy to keep an accident victim's things so that a certain hotelier, no matter how lovely, can rifle through them."

"Ah, come on, Tuck," she said, giving him a pouty smile.

"No. And that's final."

Nora felt like a child who just had her hand taken out of the cookie jar. "Okay. Maybe if you get into his computer, you could check for something that looks like a review."

Tuck picked up one of the pleather bags. "I'll be on the lookout." He leaned forward and gave her a kiss that had Nora's head spinning. "You do know that I think you're doing an excellent job with the hotel."

Nora appreciated Tuck's praise, but losing Alan Shaw's laptop was going to slow down her efforts of eliminating the damaging reviews.

Chapter 12

After Tuck left with the luggage of the unlucky Mr. Shaw, and with only an hour to go until the keynote speech, a surge of panic raced through Nora. Once again, her worries started to get the better of her. True, they had a hotel full of people, but now these guests wanted a 50 percent discount. The well-planned convention she had dreamed of was quickly slipping into a nightmare.

Val's application was still hidden in a drawer at the front desk. Nora's pride was getting the better of her. She promised herself she would show Marty Val's application the next time she spoke with her, as well as come clean with the problems going on with the convention. If she could erase the one-star reviews, then she could also destroy the rationale behind Mrs. Martin-Ortega's request for a deep discount.

Nora looked up Rate My Hotel on the office computer. How had she never been aware of this site before? Someone who had been to hotel school probably learned about it on the first day, she thought sourly. She typed in the Tunie Hotel in Piney Woods, Texas, and as she combed through each paragraph of vitriol, it was obvious to her that Alan Shaw was a born critic.

His beautifully written reviews illustrated things like moldy bathrooms and stained carpets on the upper floors. He'd never been inside a guest room, but from the tone of the reviews, it sounded as if he had lived in the hotel for a month. He should have been a novelist because the scathing reviews were pure fiction. If Nora had to guess, he was describing Hickelby's Motor Lodge. When she pulled up the "Contact Us" page, there was a phone number for their offices. She quickly dialed it in.

"Rate My Hotel. How may I help you?" A cheery voice answered.

"Yes. I was wondering what you can do if somebody falsely submits reviews to your site."

There was an audible sigh on the other end, as if this person had taken this phone call too many times. She responded in a rote fashion. "If you feel that the review was in error, you can contest it."

"How do I do that?"

"To contest a review, you need to prove that the reviewer is lying and operating in a malicious way."

Her answer was so succinct that Nora suspected she was reading it off a script.

"Just how do most people go about proving that kind of thing?"

"Well ... Most people can't prove something like that. We are a site built on opinions. It's kind of hard to contest somebody's opinion. If your reviewer had a bad day and took it out on your hotel, there isn't much you can do."

Nora tapped her fingers on the desk as she thought. "I'm calling from the Tunie Hotel in Piney Woods, Texas, and we had someone come in who didn't have a reservation and blamed it on us. When he found out we couldn't rent him a room, he became angry. We are pretty sure he put ten one-star reviews on your website. His reviews cite things that the man could have never seen. He's never been in a single guest room in our hotel, and yet he posted reviews on your site."

"I see. So, you have absolutely no record of a reservation from this guest in your system?"

"None at all. We're totally booked up and couldn't have rented him a room if we had wanted to."

"And are you sure he didn't come to your hotel and visit another guest?"

"No. This was the first we'd ever seen of him. He came here from out of town, and as far as we know, he doesn't know anybody here."

There was a clicking on a keyboard on the other side of the phone. "I'm going to have to put you on hold." Elevator music came gently into her ear.

A couple of local men in black leather vests emboldened with a serpent on the back sauntered into the lobby. Nora recognized them from Hades Alley, the local biker bar where she had applied for a job before she was hired at the Tunie.

Could it be they were here to indulge their love of kitty cats and cozy mysteries? It seemed improbable, but cat lovers were everywhere and could be little old ladies with parakeets or burly guys with prison tats.

"Can I help you?" Nora asked.

One of the men looked up, startled. It was unusual that they hadn't come directly to the front desk.

"No. We just came to enjoy your restaurant. We hear an old drinking buddy of ours runs it now."

With a full house, having traffic off the street for the restaurant would be even tougher for Wiley and his staff to accommodate. They hadn't thought to close off the restaurant this evening.

"Do you know Wiley?"

"Know him? We've picked his ass up off the floor more than a few times. Although we haven't seen much of him lately, I guess finally getting to run his own restaurant went to his head," the barrel-chested man said.

The other biker, who was much thinner than his friend, punched him in the arm. "Don't you know, man? Old Wiley got the cure. He's healed." The two men started laughing loudly.

"I don't know if this is a good night to visit. We have a convention in the hotel, and it might be hard to find a table."

"Not a problem. We just want to go in and get a little of the atmosphere. We were thinking of bringing some of our friends here." That information should have thrilled Nora as a business owner, but it didn't. It was obvious they were both thinking on the fly. Nobody cared about the atmosphere in a hotel restaurant.

"Okay. We're just setting up for our convention's keynote speaker tonight, but I'm sure that the wait staff wouldn't mind if you went in and had a look around. Have you been to the Tunie before?"

The bigger man snuffled. "Hell, yeah. Everybody's been to the Tunie." With that, they turned and went into the dining room. It was curious. If they had been to the Tunie before, why would they want to look at it now? Most of the town viewed the Tunie's changes at the guest reunion when the hotel reopened.

Still, Nora could not recall two gentlemen as rough as this engaging in the festivities. Whatever these guys were up to, she didn't have time to think about it. Now that the reviews were going to be taken down, she could tell Miss Martin-Ortega that the negative ratings were simply a malicious action and that the room rate would remain the same. The Tunie would come out in the black now, and she could tell Marty about all of it, and maybe they could share a laugh.

The elevator music stopped, and the voice on the other side returned. "Very interesting. I just looked up your hotel. The first thing that stands out to me is that we only allow one review per customer, and somehow a person with the same IP address was able to post ten reviews, all of them negative. This is expressly against our policy here at *Rate My Hotel*. I can delete all of them for you if you would like." The woman on the phone asked Nora like it was a choice she would want to consider before taking such drastic action.

Nora responded without another second. "I would like that very much. When will they be coming down?"

"I'm deleting them right now, but it still takes about twenty-four hours for the reviews to work their way out of our system. I apologize for the time lag, but that's the best we can do. Is there anything else I can help you with today at *Rate My Hotel*?"

"Nope," Nora answered triumphantly, "you've helped us more than you can know."

As Nora hung up the phone, the two bikers came back out of the dining room, walking at a fast pace toward the lobby door. She shouted to them as they rushed out onto the street. "Is that all you needed?"

"That ought to do it," the barrel-chested biker said with a grin as the lobby door closed.

The smell of the fried chicken was rising from the kitchen, so she headed over to check on Wiley and ask him what the two men wanted. Everything needed to be ready as the guests began to come down in the next half hour. Dominic had returned from his break, so Nora made her way across the carpet from the quiet dining room to the noisy cacophony of the chaotic kitchen.

"Wiley? What else goes in the potato salad?" Caesar asked.

"I told you the recipe is right up on the board. Read the recipe and don't bother me." Wiley's face was beet red, and his hair was plastered to his balding head.

"Is everything okay in here, Uncle Wiley?"

"Fine." He directed Nora," Grab those rolled silverware napkins and start putting them out on the tables."

"Sure. Hey, what did those two guys want?"

"What two guys?"

"Two old drinking buddies of yours just stopped in. You didn't speak with them?"

"Darlin, I have no idea what you're talking about. Now get the silverware on the tables." Nora went to get the tub of wrapped silverware when a large gentleman in a white button-down short-sleeved shirt walked in carrying a clip board. His face was not familiar, so Nora knew he wasn't a part of Wiley's staff. "Can I help you?" Maybe it was a guest looking to see if dinner was about to be served, Nora thought.

"You certainly can. My name is Don Jansen, and I'm from the health department. We received a call that it might be a good idea to do a spot check on your facility today."

Wiley came forward, drying his hands on a dish towel.

"Hey, Mr. Jansen. A spot check? I didn't think you fellas did that kind of thing."

"Normally, we don't, but we received a phone call that there is a possible mishandling of food at this location and that you are feeding a large crowd."

Wiley's eyebrows furrowed together. "Somebody called and said we're mishandling food."

"Yes. You don't mind an impromptu inspection, do you, Wiley? With a new kitchen like this, there can't be anything too wrong with it."

"I suppose not. Look around. We're awful busy because we have a convention in town."

"I'll stay out of your way. I should be out of here in ten minutes."

As Mr. Jansen started walking around the kitchen, looking under counters and running his finger along the cutting boards, Nora whispered into Wiley's ear. "Is this strange?"

"Very strange."

Nora looked at her watch. The guests would be down any minute.

Chapter 13

As Nora escorted the health department inspector from the kitchen, he turned back to her as he inserted his pen into his metal clipboard case. "Okay. I need to go write up my report. This shouldn't take too much longer." He gave her a quick salute and headed into the dining room.

"That didn't seem that bad," Nora said.

"Yeah. It took a lot longer when I was working for Jumbo Jim. He doesn't keep his kitchen as clean as I do."

Their eyes followed Don Jansen as he made his way through the chairs and tables in the dining room. He stopped suddenly and crouched down.

Nora whispered to Wiley. "What's he doing? Taking a knee after a good inspection?"

Wiley's eyebrows rose, and he put a hand on his chin. "I don't rightly know. It can't be so good that he's thanking his creator."

The health inspector took his pen out and fidgeted with something on the carpet. "What could be out there? He's already inspected the kitchen."

Wiley shook his head in confusion. "The dining room would be a part of his checklist, but ours is spotless."

The health inspector pulled his cell phone out of his pocket and snapped a picture of the carpet. Had one of the wait staff spilled something today? Nora had longed to put new flooring in the dining room, but it just wasn't in the budget. The carpet that had been there was installed in the eighties, and maintaining it was a full-time job. Still, though, the carpets had been cleaned last week.

Wiley's hand went to his chin as he bit his lower lip. "That really can't be good. He's documenting evidence."

Nora drew in a breath, trying to keep herself calm. She had just taken care of the negative reviews, and now they had a spot inspection by the health department? It was like they were doomed to fail, no matter what she did.

"I'd better get back to the desk. Guests are going to start coming down for dinner. Are you okay in here?"

"We're ready to go. We need to put this health department guy in the back of our minds for now. Time to make the most of today, like they teach you in AA. It's show time."

Nora liked Uncle Wiley's attitude. Staying positive was the key. She passed the area where the health department inspector had been taking a picture, but there wasn't any kind of stain on the floor. Maybe he liked the color of the carpet so much that he wanted to use it in his own home.

While Nora was in the dining room, Evangeline Cartwright had entered the lobby and stood at the counter, chatting with Max. "There you are. I just wanted to tell you what a lovely room I have." Evangeline's smile was warm and welcoming. It was a relief after all the stress Nora had been facing.

Finally, something was going right. Someone had something good to say. Not just anyone, but the keynote speaker for their first official conference at the Tunie Hotel. Tonight, Evangeline had changed into a soft maroon dress with a necklace that mixed maroon and black beads that playfully sparkled around her neck.

"Are you ready for this evening?" Nora asked.

"I believe so. I've done this type of thing a couple of times before and even have a stump speech, if you can believe it," she assured Nora.

Her glance strayed to the door. "My friend Doug said that he would meet me in the lobby. I thought he'd be here by now. I didn't want to tell him my room number. I think he's a wonderful man, but I didn't think it was very appropriate."

How cute, Nora thought. Even at their age, they were observing a days-gone-by polite behavior between single men and women. Evangeline had just met her long-time fan, and they were both up in years. The tinted glass of the lobby door opened, letting light into the lobby. Instead of it being Evangeline's gentleman caller, Izzy Franklin marched another manila envelope she held tightly to her breast. In an obvious attempt at dressing for the evening, she had added a black blazer to her frumpy-looking plaid skirt. Her eyes took on a glow when they landed on Evangeline Cartwright, standing at the counter.

"Wonderful," Izzy sang out in her nasally voice. "I was hoping I would get to see you before tonight."

"Here I am," Evangeline said with a welcoming smile, and then she pointed to Izzy's possession. "May I deduce that you are holding a new copy of your manuscript?"

"Ah, always the amateur sleuth. This manuscript is brand spanking new, fresh off the copy machine at the library."

"That must've taken a lot of dimes," Max muttered under his breath.

Izzy glared at Nora. "Yes, it did, and it was an unnecessary expense. One thing I've learned from this experience is that when I have something as valuable as a manuscript that contains my heart and soul poured out on the pages, I will always deliver it personally and never depend on others."

"Come, come now. Izzy," Evangeline said. "I heard Nora was stuck in the elevator. It was a frightening experience, to be sure. You couldn't ask her to crawl out of the shaft holding your manuscript. I'm just pleased that you could deliver a copy of it to me so quickly."

Izzy relented just a bit at Evangeline's advice. "I suppose. How long do you think it will be before you get a chance to read it?"

Evangeline was a successful author and was probably busy with work of her own. Taking the time out to read the novel of an aspiring writer could be a chore. Still, though, she continued to handle the situation with charm and grace. "I can't really say, but I absolutely promise to get to it and get back to you. Did you put your email address on the envelope?"

"Yes, Miss Cartwright. It's right there. I'll anxiously await your critique of the manuscript. Now I don't want you to go easy on me. Don't do me any favors. Let me know what needs fixing."

Max strolled over to the dining room. Normally, at this point, he would take a swing by the snack display, but Nora noticed he kept on walking.

"What, no candy bar?" Nora asked.

Max patted his stomach. "On a diet. Good for my health."

Max's stomach emitted a hollow sound, like a hungry bear growling after a long winter's nap.

The lobby door opened again as sunlight streamed in from the street. Doug Lindstrom had changed out of his usual sweater vest into a navy-blue suit with a red tie. He looked dashing, Nora thought. What had he looked like as a young man?

His eyes met Evangeline's, and he grinned. "Am I late?"

"Right on time," Evangeline said as she walked over and slipped her hand through his arm.

More guests started coming into the lobby, and Evangeline and Doug excused themselves to find their places in the banquet room. The extra wait staff, which consisted of Little Dudley from Dudley's Brew and a few of his friends, stood at the doors and politely seated the incoming Meow Meetup members.

"Looking stellar tonight, my lady," Little Dudley said in his surfer dude way of speaking. The ladies he was seating were tickled at his over-the-top descriptions.

Marty walked with a cane into the lobby in a sparkling silver pant suit that highlighted her silvery gray hair.

"You look beautiful," Max said.

"Do I? This is one of my leftovers from my real estate days."

"Let me just say, it certainly works for you. Now are you sure that ankle is ready for this evening?" Max said.

"Yes, I'm fine. I really appreciate the gossip magazines you brought me. I think I'm completely caught up on all the Hollywood starlets and their troubles." She gazed at Max, and there was a warmth to her voice. "I'll take your advice and not push it." She turned her gaze to Nora. "How is everything going? Have you had any problems today? Thank goodness I had you and Max to take care of everything. I just knew that whatever came up, you could handle it. Right, guys?"

How much of the truth was Nora willing to share with her new partner? Her answer was quick. "No problem. Everything is going fine. Just fine."

"Wonderful. I knew I could rely on you."

There was a squawk from the next room as Camille Martin-Ortega began testing the borrowed sound system Max had set up for the Meow Meetup. Her short blond curls bobbed as she kept repeating the annoying standard mic-check word, "testing ... testing." Once the crowd was seated, Mrs. Martin-Ortega announced Evangeline Cartwright, and things began progressing smoothly. Nora let out a breath she didn't know she'd been holding. Maybe she really could pull this off.

Sasha LeClaire slunk down the stairs in a black satin slip dress that hit just above the knee and clung to her athletic body. Her hair was artfully pinned up, with a few cascading strands framing her face. Most of the crowd had already assembled in the banquet room, and upon seeing Sasha, Marty whispered and gestured to the doorway, "Oh, Miss Cartwright is just about to speak. You can probably still sneak in."

Izzy was seated next to the door and was waiting for her mentor to speak. Sasha drew near the banquet room, close enough for Izzy to hear her.

"No matter. I'm going to get an interview from her anyway, and frankly, my magazine is more about the cat lover than the droll books they read. I mean, seriously, who can consider what she writes anything close to literature? Have you seen her titles? *The Cat and the Man on the Train, The Cat and the Woman Who Sang*? Not exactly Hemingway."

Izzy sat up straight now, pulling her eyes from the front to Sasha. The evil looks she'd been giving Nora for losing her manuscript had now found a new home with Sasha. Izzy rose from her chair and stamped into the lobby. Her cheeks puffed out, and her face had taken on a deep red tinge. "How dare you say such mean things about Evangeline. She is the best writer in the whole damn library, and you'll regret saying that."

Marty stepped forward to Izzy. "It's so wonderful to have Miss Cartwright's fans here. Izzy, why don't you go and enjoy some of that delicious fried chicken? It ought to be out any minute." Giving one final scowl to Sasha, Izzy returned to the banquet room.

"My, my. Some people are really uptight around here. Of course, when your entire social life is built around cats and books," Sasha said it in her slow, practiced tone.

Izzy didn't hear Sasha's last comment because the applause for Evangeline had drowned her out. As Evangeline started speaking, Nora kept checking on the computer to see if any of the one-star reviews had disappeared, even though she knew it could take up to twenty-four hours. Working on the definition of "within" twenty-four hours, Nora hoped it was really a much shorter amount of time it took to delete the reviews, so she kept refreshing the screen. Unfortunately, they kept coming back each time. Just as Nora was worried she'd be giving a discount, Evangeline started talking about the hotel.

"And I'm sure you are all bowled over by getting to stay at the historic Tunie Hotel. When I found out I was coming to Texas, I was fascinated that we would be a part of the great history of this state. The Tunie Hotel has been here through the oil boom and bust. They handled the wildcatters, and now they have wonderful members of the Meow Meetup. Not so wild, but definitely cat lovers. Let's have a big round of applause for our excellent hosts at the Tunie." The crowd responded enthusiastically. Camille Martin-Ortega's lips thinned, and her hands barely moved. Maybe things would work out and they would survive this convention? Nora began to feel silly for doubting herself. The meal went on without a hitch.

Marty, who had been in and out of the banquet room, came and patted Nora on the back. "Excellent work, partner. I should sprain my ankle more often."

"Really?" Nora couldn't let her go on. "I have to be honest with you. I've felt a little out of my element with all of this. You know, I have so little experience in hotel management."

"I'm just as unqualified as you are, but that hasn't stopped either of us. Maybe now that Val has applied, we will feel more confident."

"Oh, you saw her application?" Nora thought she had done an excellent job of hiding it in the desk, but Marty had found it. She tried to sound excited, but it just wasn't happening for her. "Dominic told me about it. An application and now a successful convention. Things are turning around for us. I'm just glad we'll be able to pay the bills this month. Having your investment has really helped, but it won't be long before we're back where we were when you showed up."

"Hopefully," Nora whispered, "the Meow Meetup will have us paying our bills on time for a while."

Don Jansen, the health inspector, returned to the lobby. Nora had completely forgotten about him. "Sorry. I got called away on an emergency. Slime in the ice machine, you know. I do have your report. Would you like me to share it with you or with your restaurant manager?"

Marty cocked her head to the side. "We were inspected? Why didn't you tell me?"

The health inspector nodded. "Yes, ma'am. Surprise spot inspection, and frankly, I'm pretty glad someone called me."

Marty slipped him a curious glance. "Do you know who that was?"

"It was an anonymous tip. Your kitchen checked out just fine. It's one of the cleanest kitchens I've seen in this area. Your dining room, though, was another matter."

Nora remembered that he had looked at something on the floor. "We have a regular cleaning schedule for the carpet."

"The floor was clean. I'll give you that. The little critter running around on it was not so clean. I cited you for cockroaches." He ripped off his report and handed it to Nora and Marty.

"We haven't had cockroaches here for months. I made sure the place was fumigated when I renovated it," Marty said.

"Nevertheless, you had a couple of the little guys today. That's all that matters. I'll be writing this up, and it will be posted on the website for our consumers. Have a nice day."

Nora put her palms on her forehead in frustration. Once again, the minute she thought she could relax, something else happened. "I can't believe it."

"Believe it." Max said as he returned to the computer at the front desk. "Sometimes I think somebody is out to get us."

"I promise you, Marty. I'll find out how we ended up with cockroaches," Nora said. "I'll do everything I can to make this right. This is going to be a success. I promise."

Nora expected much worse from Marty, but she was calm. "I know, dear, I know. I just hope none of them crawl into our guest's food. What if they start asking for a discount?"

Nora shuddered. They certainly might.

Max interrupted. "Uh oh."

"What?" Nora snapped.

Max pointed to his computer screen. "The Google alert just came up for the Tunie." Max had put up a Google alert for any time the words "Tunie Hotel" were featured anywhere. This way, they'd know if they were written up by a travel writer or blog. "That's great!" Marty was excited to see the news.

"Maybe, maybe not. It seems Mr. Shaw submitted one final article to a site named Travel Tippers before he died. It's all about the Tunie. He titled it *The Scourge of the South: Staying in a Sleazy Hotel in Piney Woods, Texas.*"

"Mr. Shaw?" Marty asked. "You mean the man who died in the elevator shaft? Why would he leave a negative review?" After how well Marty handled the cockroach situation, Nora knew it was time to tell her about what kind of person Alan Shaw really was.

Chapter 14

As Nora, Max, and Marty leaned over the computer, they read Alan Shaw's last words.

The Tunie Hotel is indeed an establishment of the old West.

The old West in the way of inadequate lodgings, a terrible smell, and out-of-date furnishings. No wonder cowboys are always shooting one another. Just between you and me, I feel much safer on the East Coast, where I can find "larning" and civilization.

His words were witty and malicious at the same time. He had a way of building a sense of comradery with his audience, and whoever read the article would immediately feel a partnership with him if they'd ever stayed in a bad hotel. He did have a gift with words, but unfortunately, his talent might destroy the Tunie Hotel and Nora and Marty's investment.

Marty, who had pulled out her reading glasses to focus on the computer screen, asked, "Didn't they fact-check this?"

Max chuckled. "Yeah, right. This is what they call sensational travel writing. The underbelly of the hospitality industry. How many times can you say the Grand Canyon is majestic? This is the stuff that sells ads. Because of Mr. Shaw, we have an awful hotel that the reader is now thankful to know about before they plan their long-awaited trip to Texas."

Nora picked up the phone. At least she could take care of this in front of Marty and prove her worth. "I'm going to call them for a retraction. They must have noticed he didn't submit any photos."

Max tapped on the mouse. "No, wait. Let me scroll down. There's one." At the bottom of the page was a picture of a ceiling. It had a nasty water stain on it that was the size of an area rug.

"We don't have any rooms with stains like that, do we?" Nora asked. "I didn't think we had any water damage at the Tunie."

"We don't!" Marty exclaimed, her voice filled with frustration.

Nora's anger grew with each passing moment. "Then where did he get a picture like this?"

Max scratched his head. "You ladies are making the mistake of thinking the photograph is legitimate. All he had to do was find a water-stained ceiling on the internet and submit it as his own."

Marty shook her head in disgust. "And I repeat, why didn't this magazine fact-check this? Did anyone get a call from Travel Tippers?"

"I didn't," Nora said.

"Neither did I," Max added.

"Max, I know we can't sue Alan Shaw, but is there anything we can do to sue this magazine?" Marty asked.

Max fairly beamed that Marty was turning to him to help her solve this problem. He was studying to be a lawyer, but because he lived in a small town without a law school, he was pursuing his degree online. Even with that shaky credential, Max had become the hotel's legal counsel. "I believe you have grounds for a very good case here, especially if you can prove that this untruthful article cost you money."

Indeed, it was about to cost the hotel money if Nora agreed to give the Meow Meetup organizer, Camille Martin-Ortega, a 50 percent discount on their room rentals for the weekend.

During their conversation, Sasha LeClaire had returned to the counter and was now tapping her sleek black fingernails across the wood surface. Her matching black stiletto heels were graced with rhinestones on the straps, and her hair was in an elegant French roll with more rhinestones placed throughout. There was a look of casual chic about it as graceful strands framed her face. "Excuse me."

Nora looked up. "I'm sorry, we were having a little crisis here. How can I help you?"

She waved her hand in the air as if brushing off Nora like a gnat in the summer. "Whatever. I was wondering if it was all right when the guests leave the keynote speech if you could siphon them over my way for interviews and photos for our Facebook page."

"I guess we could do that." Nora wasn't too sure how the guests would feel about being "siphoned," but she was trying to be hospitable. "Why don't you stand right over there?" Nora gestured to the area in front of what they called the snack shop, which was really an alcove with a bunch of shelves. Sasha LeClaire took one look at it and turned her nose up. It was obviously not what she had in mind.

"I think I should be a little closer to the door. Trust me, they're all going to be running out of there after this boring speech they've been enduring from this has-been cozy mystery writer. Seriously, this is who they hired as their keynote speaker? There are dozens of cat veterinarians or breeders who would have been so much more suitable. I thought we were here because of our common interest in cats, not paperback books." She said the last part with great disdain, as if reading books was something only the lower classes did.

Hearing this negative appraisal of Evangeline Cartwright, Nora's eyes dashed to Izzy, who still sat by the door. She began to flinch as Sasha continued to insult Evangeline.

"I mean, seriously, who reads those kinds of books?" Sasha continued, unaware of Izzy's mounting anger. "If I had arranged this convention, I certainly would have had someone who would discuss cat breeding and pedigrees. Indulging in a fantasy with some two-bit hack is just... infantile."

Storm clouds were gathering above Izzy's head, and before Nora could warn Sasha, the librarian had stepped out of the banquet room and yanked Sasha around to face her.

"How dare you! How dare you insult Evangeline Cartwright again? What is your problem with her?" Izzy squeaked.

"I have no problem with her. I simply find her annoying. I'm here to get pictures of some of the guests. Would you like to be featured on our Facebook page?"

Between the discounting of Izzy's emotions and the condescending Facebook ploy, Max and Marty moved closer.

"Oh, you think you're so special with your purry voice and your beautiful clothes," Izzy said, sputtering the P in purry. Izzy, in her boxy blazer, had her hair cut in a functional short bob that made her ears stick out just a bit.

Where Sasha had artfully applied makeup, Izzy had applied none. Her plain brown eyes, framed by the deep lenses of her glasses, registered deep anger at the woman who insulted her favorite author. "You want to get pictures of people? Take a picture of this, cat lady. Your website has overpriced cat products on it that nobody wants. And this may shock you, but cats do not need bottled water and gourmet food. Especially not at the prices you charge. You may as well pack up your skinny ass and leave. You are not wanted here."

While waiting for Sasha's comeback, Nora held her breath. Instead of trading insults with the mousy librarian, Sasha merely knocked her head back and laughed. She didn't laugh just once, but for several seconds. The more she laughed, the angrier Izzy became. Before anybody could stop her, Izzy reached over to a Meow Meetup cardboard poster that rested on a tripod and slammed it over Sasha's head, knocking her to the floor. Once Sasha was down, Izzy continued to pummel her with the heavy cardboard display, uttering oaths with every slam. It was like she had violated the "no noise in the library" rule and kept violating it over and over again.

Just as the tension was building, Tuck walked in, clueless about the unfolding events, and immediately began apologizing to Nora for his tardiness. "I'm finally here. Sorry, I got busy with the investigation." His eyes drifted to Izzy, with Sasha flattened on the carpet as she repeatedly hit her with the industrial-grade cardboard featuring her heroine, Evangeline Cartwright. Tuck ran over, picked up Izzy under the arms, and shifted her sturdy little body off Sasha.

Sasha rose slightly, yet seductively, off the floor. "Oh, thank you, kind sir. This woman is insane. She attacked me right here in the lobby. You are my knight in shining armor." Sasha batted her eyes at Tuck with an appreciative grin.

Tuck nodded roughly and then sat Izzy on one of the red velvet benches up against the historic picture wall. "Miss Franklin? What is going on here? You know, if you had told me two weeks ago that nice lady from behind the checkout desk would act like this, I never would've believed you."

Izzy lifted her chin resolutely and said, "This woman is rude and mean, and she was insulting Evangeline Cartwright."

Most of the banquet crowd had stopped listening to Evangeline several minutes ago when the noise picked up in the lobby. The convention goers now crowded in the doorway.

Evangeline still stood at the podium with a look of concern on her face.

Tuck advised patiently, "That doesn't mean you have to hit her."

"I know," she sighed as her shoulders began to sag. "She wouldn't stop, and I don't know, something just went off in me, and I wanted to hit her. Then I wanted to hit her again, and that felt so good, so I did it again. I know it was entirely inappropriate," Izzy confessed, now looking down at the floor.

Sasha gracefully ran her hands through her hair. With just a slight jostle, the strands that had come loose from her hair made her look even more alluring. "Thank you so much, Tuck," she drawled. "You just never know what kind of people will come to these conventions." She glanced at the crowd gathered at the door and plastered on a fake smile as her red lips split over perfectly white teeth. "Not you folks, of course. As soon as your lovely and talented keynote speaker finishes, I would love a few of you to come see me so I can take your picture for our Facebook page, the Cat Aficionado website. That's CatAficionado.com."

Tuck's focus was on Izzy. "Miss Franklin, I'm going to need to have a few words with you. I was planning on talking to you anyway when I heard you had an altercation with Alan Shaw the night of his death."

"Alan Shaw? Oh. The reporter who was being so nasty? What happened to him was very unfortunate, but I put him in his place. That's all." She quietly folded her hands in her lap, resuming the persona of the quiet librarian.

Tuck observed Izzy. "I see. And just how angry were you with Mr. Shaw?"

Doug Lindstrom made his way through the crowd and came over to Izzy and Tuck. "Mr. Shaw was exceedingly rude," he stated. "You were there. You saw how he was acting. I don't know why you need to question this lady. She was simply there talking about her manuscript to her favorite writer when this man barged in. There's not much more to it. Besides, she wasn't the only one who was angry with him that night."

Tuck nodded, acknowledging Doug's point. "Yes, but she's the only one who slapped him. Miss Franklin, can I ask you your whereabouts the night that Alan Shaw died?" A collective gasp went up across the room.

Izzy Franklin's mood had turned in an instant. She choked out her words. "I was at home asleep."

"Alone?"

Izzy's face flushed red. "Of course, alone. I'm not married."

"No boyfriends? Girlfriends?"

"Of course not!" Izzy was shocked at the assumptions that Tuck was making. She obviously didn't have either sex staying over with her. Her life seemed to be more involved with books and writing, not booty calls.

"I thought Alan Shaw's death was being called an accident. Why are you asking these questions?" Izzy asked.

"Just a matter of procedure," Tuck answered quickly.

"I would like to press charges against this woman," Sasha said as she drew near to the group.

"What for?" Izzy asked flatly.

Sasha tilted her head to the side and smiled slowly. "Assault, my dear. You just don't go attacking people and expect to get away with it."

Izzy rose to advance on Sasha once again, but Tuck took her by the arm. "Why don't both of you come back with me to the police station? We're right next door, and I'm sure we can get this all sorted out. Also, I have a few more questions to ask you, Mrs. Franklin."

"Miss."

"Miss."

Tuck worked to separate the little librarian as she drew closer to Sasha LeClaire. Could Izzy have pushed Alan Shaw down the elevator shaft? What was it that caused Alan Shaw to become such a bulldog when it came to Evangeline Cartwright? Nora tried to remember his words the last time she saw him.

I know who you are, sweetie.

Who did he think she was?

Chapter 15

As Tuck began dragging Izzy out, she uttered her final words to the gathered crowd of Meow Meetup attendees. "It's all for Evangeline. Why are people so against her when she does such wonderful things for others? I will protect Evangeline for the rest of my days if she needs me to do that. Go ahead. Bring on the jail time. I don't care. This world has few people like Evangeline in it. God bless her. I would give my kidney to her if she needed it." Her voice trailed off into the noise of the street as she was dragged out the door. Evangeline, who had witnessed the entire scene, was now standing uncomfortably at the podium.

She put her hand on her heart and smiled graciously.

Nora stepped before the crowd. "Talk about a fan. I don't believe Evangeline is at the end of her speech, and I can't promise you anything quite as exciting, but if you will join her back in the banquet room, she'll do her best." The assembled members of the group murmured and returned to their chairs.

"I sure didn't see that coming," Max said.

Marty scratched her head. "What kind of books does she write?"

"Mysteries."

"It's a mystery to me why our town librarian is willing to part with vital organs for her," Max remarked.

Marty and Max had not witnessed the scene in the dining room with Alan Shaw, so Nora tried to explain. "Izzy had been a fan of her work as she worked in the library, but Evangeline's kind gesture of offering to read Izzy's manuscript was enough to make her a friend for life. I don't know what it is about this woman, but people are extremely loyal to her."

As Evangeline began talking again, Doug Lindstrom stood in the doorway of the banquet hall, looking out into the lobby. He stepped over to Nora. "You handled that beautifully," he said in a whisper.

"What was I going to do? I had to get her off Miss LeClaire. I hope it wasn't too disruptive to Miss Cartwright."

He stepped closer to Nora and leaned forward. "I think she will be fine. If anything, it gives the convention goers a wonderful story to tell when they get back home. There are so many situations here at the hotel. It may surprise you, but not everybody is built to act on instinct. It is our instincts that can save lives."

"Did you learn that from working with dogs?"

He laughed and then quieted down, looking at the banquet room. They were still rapt with attention to the speech. "Some of it," he said in a lower voice. "I just wanted to thank you for trying to keep everything under control. I know you've done a lot of work here, and this is the biggest event our little Tunie has had in decades. I think you and Marty have pulled this off beautifully."

Nora felt a little embarrassed by the dog trainer's comments. She didn't feel that way, but it was comforting to know that the running of the convention looked good to an outsider. Even though Doug Lindstrom was thirty years her senior, he was a very handsome man. Could he be flirting with her? Nora quickly brushed the thought out of her mind. He seemed to be dedicated to Evangeline. It struck Nora that this was yet another person swearing allegiance to the strange mystery writer.

"Thanks," Nora acknowledged. "Lately, I haven't always felt that way, so your words are coming at a good time for me."

"It's tough to have an idea that nobody else believes in. It's even tougher to implement a plan to bring it forth. I was sure the Tunie was going to be knocked down by a wrecking ball one day. It was going to be another piece of lost Texas history, but here we are, having a lovely meal and listening to my favorite writer. With the improvements you and your partner have made to the property by bringing this old place into this century with modern technology, it has gone from being the town's eyesore to one of its proudest accomplishments. You know I heard all about what happened with Mr. Brockwell. He was the epitome of *the man,* if you know what I mean."

"I would have appreciated meeting you when I first came to town."

"That's kind of you to say. It's tough moving to a new town. All I remember when I first came to Piney Woods was that Adam Brockwell was the establishment around here. Nobody ever questions the good old boys of Texas. Am I right?" The dog trainer's face flushed, revealing he did not have a high opinion of Adam Brockwell. Doug's eyes drifted to Evangeline, who was about to finish her talk.

"How long have you known Miss Cartwright?" Nora asked.

Doug pressed his lips together and sighed. "Oh, a long, long time. I mean, through her books."

Applause went up as Evangeline finished her speech.

"I better get going. It was nice talking to you, and again, thanks for keeping the peace around here." A smile came to his eyes. "I thought that was your boyfriend's job."

"I help out where I can."

Doug returned to the banquet room and joined Evangeline at her table. Nora noticed Doug's hand quietly slipping over Evangeline's. Would she and Tuck be holding hands at that age? Would they even be together by then? Nora started thinking of Sasha LeClaire. For the first time since she'd been in Piney Woods and with Tuck, she felt jealous. Sasha was just so good at flirting with him. It was becoming obvious that there was some sort of chemistry between Tuck and Sasha.

Then again, maybe her boyfriend was just reacting like any red-blooded American male. Nora glanced over at Evangeline and Doug once more.

There was so much more to these two people than what she knew. She could feel it.

Chapter 16

After everything settled down, Marty and Max decided to have dinner together in the dining room.

Nora was happy for Max, but Alan Shaw was on her mind. She had only spoken to the man twice, each time for less than five minutes. How could one person do so much damage in so little time? Even more important, who else's life had he messed up so quickly that they pushed him down the elevator shaft? He had never set foot in Piney Woods before, but Texans were famous for shooting first and asking questions later.

Nora had so looked forward to this convention, but after everything that had happened, she could not wait until the last guest in their mangy little cat sweatshirt went home. After dinner, Max had returned to his home, which he shared with his mother, and Marty returned to her fourth-floor apartment stating she wanted to get off her foot after such an exciting evening.

Nora worked alone at the check-in desk, and her long to-do list was finally coming to an end. She pulled up Alan Shaw's magazine but didn't see any other articles he had written. The online version of *Cat Lover* didn't have Alan Shaw's name anywhere. He wasn't a feature writer, and that surprised her. What about that secretary he said he had? Maybe he was on the editorial staff? She searched again, but Nora came up with nothing. Whoever Alan Shaw was, he didn't work for this magazine. Nora put Alan's name in a general internet search box. The list that came up was pages long. There was an Alan Shaw who owned a bowling alley in New Jersey, and another who seemed to be the father of pickles. She finally had some luck when she searched under Alan Shaw, reporter. A series of articles came up in a magazine titled *First Reporter* on a wastewater facility that was ruining the environment. The same way he had attacked the Tunie, Alan had attacked the environmental disaster. His words were like arrows as they reached their point. The wastewater facility ended up making significant changes, possibly due to his reporting.

The injustices spilled out through this community's waterways should not go unpunished, and this reporter will be sure that the powers that be take care of it.

Nora searched for the magazine that had published the wastewater article and found he had several stories there, along with other magazines he had worked for. Instead of being attached to one magazine, Alan Shaw was a freelance investigative reporter. He worked for whoever would pay him. Most of his pieces were about helping the common man. Nora sat back in her chair, listening to the dishes and silverware clink in the next room as Wiley's staff finished serving the few stray guests that had come in after the banquet crowd left.

What in the world would Alan Shaw be investigating in Piney Woods, Texas?

There were several other articles where Alan Shaw searched out investigative stories and brought those he perceived as criminals to justice. He went after a man who bred pit bulls and shut him down. He rescued an old lady who was losing her home because of the rigorous rules and fees of a homeowner's association.

What could be attracting a guy like Alan Shaw here at the Meow Meetup? Why would he want to interview Evangeline? Nora could not think of what this charming woman would have done to get a man like Alan Shaw tracking her. Maybe it was just a standard interview he was doing to pay the rent? If Nora wanted to know what her intrepid reporter had been doing, she needed to either access the laptop that was in the possession of the police department or figure out what magazine he was really working for and where he planned to pitch Evangeline's interview. Nora pulled up several articles and found that six of them were at the First Reporter. It was nearly eight thirty in the evening. Even investigative reporters left the office eventually. Nevertheless, she found a phone number for the offices and gave it a ring. "First Reporter, your news just might be news."

"Hi. I'm surprised to find anybody working so late."

"Yeah, as I said. Your news might be news, and on a slow news day, I'm open to all possibilities." This time, the voice didn't sound quite so canned.

"I was wondering if you could tell me anything about Alan Shaw."

"Alan? That dog. What's he done now? He's at the end of the legal fees we're willing to pay for him. Make sure he knows that." It sounded like Mr. Shaw had worn out his welcome at First Reporter. Maybe all that justified snooping was just a bit illegal at times.

"No. He hasn't done anything. It's what's been done to him. Can you tell me, was he on an assignment for your magazine?"

There was the squeak of an office chair on the other end of the line. "Whoa, whoa, whoa. Let's just back this up a bit. What do you mean something was done to him?"

It seemed the night desk employee at the First Reporter didn't miss a thing. Nora debated how to inform this person of Alan Shaw's death. It was hard to believe the man at the bottom of the elevator had any close friends, but who knew? "This is Nora Alexander calling from Piney Woods, Texas. He said he was here for Cat Lover Magazine. I am starting to believe he was working on another story. We have a convention called the Meow Meetup at our hotel right now."

"Seriously? That's what it's called? Is this where people with cats meet up? Like on dates?"

"I didn't name it. Were you good friends with Mr. Shaw?"

"It's difficult for anyone to be friends with Alan. What do you mean, *were*? Has something happened to him?"

Nora blew out a sigh. "Mr. Shaw had a terrible accident and fell down the elevator shaft. We thought he worked for *Cat Lover Magazine*, but I couldn't find any connection between Mr. Shaw and the publication. Now we are having a tough time trying to find anyone who actually knew him."

The man on the other end of the line blew out a whistle. "Damn. Are you kidding?" Even though the night desk voice had been impartial before this, now he sounded almost sad.

"No. I'm so sorry."

"How in the hell did he fall down an elevator shaft?"

"It was blocked off, but the doors to the empty shaft were open, but still we found him dead at the bottom. We really aren't sure what happened yet."

"As in, the police are investigating this? Is this an accident or was it murder?"

"We're not sure of that either. Right now, it's being classified as an accident."

"Holy cow. I've got to call the boss."

Nora could feel she was about to be hung up on. She'd given all the information in this phone call and not received any. "Hold on one minute. Was Alan Shaw working for your magazine?"

"Why do you care?"

Nora stammered. "He died in my hotel. He came in here lying to us from the get-go, and I would like to know why."

"So, you say you're somewhere in Texas? Dallas? Was that it?"

"No, I'm in Piney Woods. We are in East Texas, close to the Louisiana border. This is the Tunie Hotel. Was he working for you or not?"

"Alan Shaw." The tone of the voice on the other end again changed as he took a pause. "If he was, he was probably working on one of his half-assed conspiracy theories. He didn't even think we landed on the moon, that guy. Let me look through my file." There was a shuffling on the other end, and then the night desk reporter came back on the phone. "It looks like he did pitch an idea because he asked for travel expenses. I'm surprised he even remembered to turn in the form. Shaw could be forgetful, so this is unusual. I was never sure if he just forgot to turn in his requests or if he felt like he didn't have to."

"What was the idea?"

"I can't really tell. He just said he was going to unearth the biggest story since Watergate. What did he tell you he was there for?"

"To interview our keynote speaker, who is a mystery writer."

"Huh?"

"I know what you mean. It doesn't make any sense."

"I have to call my boss. I might be heading your way. Save a room in your hotel for Rick Stephenson."

"That might be tough."

"Ah yes, the Meow Meetup. Are you sure it isn't some kind of singles thing?"

"It's a convention for cat lovers. Mostly older women, but some men. No one here seems like they're looking to hook up, only talk about the world of cats." As the words came out of Nora's mouth, she considered Sasha LeClaire. Everybody but one was.

"Seriously? If Alan was so desperate that he was investigating little old ladies with cats, he wasn't pushed. He jumped."

Chapter 17

When Nora finally left the Tunie Hotel at about 11:30 and returned to the Piney Woods Bed and Breakfast, she was too wired to go to sleep. Between the many tasks of managing a convention and Alan Shaw's death, her mind would not stop replaying the day. To try to find a sense of calm, Nora made a cup of hot cocoa with Tatty's special combination of cocoa, sugar, and a little cinnamon. She took her steaming mug to the front porch swing and pushed her heels back and forth, causing a comfortable squeak. Nora snuggled into her soft tan cashmere sweater and looked up at the stars in the clear night sky. The evening air soothed her. She breathed in and closed her eyes. She had to be back at work early tomorrow, so getting relaxed enough to sink into quality sleep tonight was important.

"Nora?" Tuck spoke softly from where he stood on the bottom step of the porch. "Are you awake?"

Nora's eyelids opened at his gentle voice, and she felt a warm rush of pleasure at seeing Tuck. She just had to hope she wasn't dreaming. She sat up in the swing and opened her eyes. "Tuck? What are you doing here?"

Tuck's smile played on the corners of his lips. "It looks like your day was as long as mine. I was driving home from work and saw you on the porch. I was a little worried you were sleeping out here. You do have your rent paid up, don't you? Because if you don't, I have a little extra room at my place." He winked.

Nora patted the seat next to her. "Come sit down with me. I wasn't asleep, but I was on my way. Can I get you some hot chocolate?"

"No. I'm fine. How are you?" He asked her like someone would ask a friend after a tragedy. Indeed, they had both been through a tragedy with the death of Alan Shaw, even if she did not particularly care for the man.

Nora yawned. "I think I've reached a new level of exhaustion. Ever get so tired you were afraid you wouldn't fall asleep?"

Tuck laughed softly and put his arm around Nora, and the two of them huddled under the stars, making the swing rock together. "I can't be too sure, but maybe that's what success feels like? Congratulations. You've done it. This is the busiest the Tunie has been in years."

"I know. It's a wonderful thing, but when I wished for a full hotel, I had no idea so many things could go wrong. Did you know the head of the Meow Meetup wants a discount? Then we think Alan Shaw left us a slew of one-star reviews we had to get rid of, and now we find out he wrote an article slamming the Tunie. How could he be so mean after such a brief encounter with our hotel?"

"That's the nature of things these days. If you have a gripe with anybody, you can just go online and tear them apart. The problem is that nobody validates the complainer. It's so easy to leave a scathing review. Any coward can shoot their mouth off and not have to worry about any type of retribution. The one-star reviews are just that."

"The only problem was that the organizer of the convention took Shaw's words as the truth, and now she wants half off the price of the rooms. She thinks she's the victim of false advertising, but really, we're the victims. Have you figured anything else out about Alan Shaw?"

"Not much."

"I was trying to determine who he was writing his article for. I ended up talking with a man named Rick Stephenson, who worked at a magazine that did investigative journalism. He knew who Alan Shaw was. I looked up Stephenson's picture online. Handsome guy."

Tuck perked up at that comment. "Handsome guy?"

"Oh, you know, it was a headshot. Everybody looks good in a headshot."

"That may be so, but it is alarming to hear my girlfriend talk about another man's headshot."

Nora attempted to change the subject. "Did you go through Mr. Shaw's laptop?"

"Yes. That part was kind of unusual. This guy had tons of books on things like aliens and moon landings. He was a real nut job."

"He was a conspiracy theorist."

Tuck, who had his arm resting comfortably around Nora, now turned to face her. She was sure he would go in for a kiss, but he pulled away in surprise. "How did you know that?"

"Rick told me."

"Rick told you?" Tuck pulled away at Nora's casual use of the reporter's first name. "Why didn't you call me?"

"You're right. I should have called, but I was just so busy with everything going on. Whatever he was here in Piney Woods for had nothing to do with cats." Nora let out a big yawn and pulled Tuck back to rest deeper into his shoulder.

"Did you find any documents about what he was here doing?" She murmured.

"No. All of his document files were empty."

This was strange. Everybody had document files on their computer. How could somebody who wrote for a living not have documents written by him? "What do you mean empty?"

"His e-book library was full, but his actual documents, the kind of thing you would create in Word, weren't there. Whatever he was writing, he wasn't keeping it on that computer."

"And then we're back to square one. He said he wanted to interview Evangeline. This is the kind of guy who spends his time investigating wastewater plants. What is there about a mystery novelist that would intrigue him?" Nora yawned again, feeling the warmth of the hot chocolate and the presence of Tuck relax her.

"The writer? That doesn't make any sense. I'll talk to Miss Cartwright tomorrow to see if she knows any reason an investigative reporter would want to talk to her. Do you think you could set that up for me?" As Tuck looked down, Nora's eyes had closed, and she had fallen asleep. He kissed her on the forehead and settled back to look at the stars.

Tatty stood in the doorway in her pink bathrobe. "I thought I heard someone out here," she whispered. "She's asleep. Poor dear. It's been quite a crazy few days for her."

"Yes, it has." He whispered, but their words were not waking the exhausted Nora up. "I was just about to ask if she could set up an interview with her mystery writer tomorrow, but she was already out."

Tatty's eyes flashed in interest. "Why do you want to interview her? Do you think she did it?"

Tuck smiled and shook his head. "No, but for some reason, our victim wanted to interview her."

"I don't think she did it." Tatty pulled the flaps of her robe up to keep out the coolness in the evening air. "She has a trustworthy face. You know what I mean?"

"Interestingly, that is not how I screen my suspects. Always remember, some people are experts at lying."

"No. There's just something about her face. This is going to sound funny, but it's almost as if I've seen her before."

"Have you read her books?"

"No, I don't think so. When you get to be my age, you aren't always sure what novels you've read, but she seems so familiar to me."

Tuck's phone buzzed in his pocket. Nora's eyes came open, and upon seeing Tatty, she smiled and pulled away from Tuck.

He answered the call efficiently. "Tuck Watson, okay. Okay."

He ended the call. "I have to go." He gave Nora a quick kiss. "Get some rest, sleeping beauty."

Nora yawned. "Are you going back to work?"

"Yes, but I'll be thinking about you the whole time."

Chapter 18

The next morning, when Nora went into work, she found Caesar pacing back and forth across the lobby, muttering to himself. Wiley had brought Caesar on board when Jumbo Jim fired him after finding out about his allegiance to his runaway gumbo cook. The two men had shared a kitchen for years, and Caesar was glad to get out from under the greasy thumbs of Jumbo Jim.

"What is the matter, Caesar? Is Wiley okay?"

"I don't know. I haven't seen him since last night. He left even before we finished cleaning up. He was very upset."

This was not what Nora wanted to hear. Today the convention offered classes, panels, and shopping for the convention goers all within the hotel. The restaurant would need to provide breakfast, lunch, and dinner. Caesar was Wiley's right-hand man, but Nora wasn't sure if he could handle running the restaurant without his boss.

"Did you try to call him?"

"Yes. I've been calling him all night. I was hoping that when I came in this morning, he'd be here. He's always the first person here."

There was an obvious conclusion about her uncle's behavior. Had the stress of the convention caused Wiley to fall off the wagon and return to his unhealthy drinking habits? She felt guilty for all the responsibility she had heaped on him selfishly, not taking into consideration that when she met him, he was deep in the throes of addiction. He had been sober longer in the last year than he had been in the last twenty years.

"Have you called his son, Vernon?" Vernon had stuck by his dad even through the worst relapses. He worked at the Brockwell Distribution Center and had tried to be there for him. Even though his dad didn't try AA until late in his life, Vernon admitted to Nora that he started out in Alateen and worked his way into the adult group. Vernon was a big strapping guy with a warm heart, and what seemed like a fountain of unlimited patience for his dad.

"Yes. I spoke to Vernon last night. He was going to search the bars for him." Wiley's favorite waterhole had always been Hades Alley, but there were a few even seedier establishments now on the edge of town. This was assuming that Wiley wasn't passed out somewhere other than a bar. Caesar continued his rant. "I just got off the phone with Vernon, and he couldn't find him. We didn't get our shipment this morning from Moore Foods. They say they lost our order."

Nora was beginning to feel like a hamster on a wheel of management problems. "I'll call Val. She'll straighten this out."

"That's not going to work. Moore Foods fired Val when they found out she applied for a job here."

"You're kidding me. Who told them?"

"I think she did. She must have really hated that job with all the shady stuff they were doing. I guess she told them she put in an application somewhere else." Caesar shook his head.

Nora ran her hand through her hair, pushing the auburn strands away from her eyes. She had opted to wear it long today and not pull it up into a ponytail. After everything that happened so far during the convention, she almost felt relaxed when she was getting ready this morning. Now she realized it was silly to relax until this group departed. "Okay, what are you doing for breakfast this morning?"

"We made pancakes. We had everything we needed. Wiley planned it out for us. He's a good boss like that. I just wish he were here right now."

"I know. Maybe it's nothing. I've been leaning on him a lot lately. Just keep flipping those flapjacks, and I'm going to try to find Wiley."

Nora found Max hunched over the computer in the office, finishing up his nightly bookkeeping duties. He had ditched the three-piece suit, and this morning he was dressed in a polo shirt and khaki pants, his go-to wardrobe.

Dominic was also in attendance. Each night, he liked to set out tiny sound recording machines to try to pick up spirits having conversations. He called these little machines EVP recorders. Electronic voice phenomenon.

"Any ghosts?" Nora inquired.

"I don't know yet. It takes me hours to listen to this stuff. Here's hoping we got us a great big ghost." He placed the recorders in a black leather bag. "I'll be here a little later to do my shift."

Even though Dominic worked a shift at the hotel, he still had time for his passion, which consisted of hours-long recordings of what would be background noise to anyone else. "Any chance you had one of those things set up on the fourth floor when Alan Shaw fell to his death?"

"I only have three recorders, and that night I had them all set up in the banquet room. Sorry," Dominic answered. "See you later." He waved as he exited the hotel.

Max started packing up his belongings as Nora took her place behind the desk. "It looks like Marty will be back in action today. I checked on her during the night, and she seems to have recovered nicely." Max was good like that. He was a giant of a man with a warm heart and an even kinder soul. Marty was lucky to have him, even if it was only a friendship.

"You did, huh?" Nora winked at him. "And how often do you go up to her apartment at night?"

Max blushed. "Almost never. Gee, Nora, you make me feel like I'm in junior high again."

"Can you blame me? You confessed to this undying love for Marty, and then I have to watch you not do anything about it?"

"I know. I'm trying, but I'm not much of a Romeo type. I guess I never got much practice. Did you notice we had dinner together last night?"

"I certainly did."

Max's humbleness was one of the things that Nora particularly liked about him. "Did you hear about Wiley?"

Nora asked as she plopped down in one of the black, padded office chairs.

Max yawned. "Sure did. Caesar's been here since five. How did you get him to stop wearing out the carpet in the lobby?"

"I sent him off to make more pancakes. Wiley left a schedule for them to follow, so we're good until that runs out."

Max patted his ample belly. "Pancakes. The first stop will be the dining room. A few stacks can't hurt my diet too much. So, no word on Wiley? I was hoping Vernon would find him."

"Nothing. Did you talk to Wiley last night?"

"No. When I came in, Wiley was deep in conversation with your half brother, Corey."

Nora winced. Corey? The last thing Lucy had told her was that Cory was going down fast. Nora expected to hear her half brother was either arrested or dead. She didn't expect him to hang out with Wiley. Wiley couldn't stand Cory and didn't trust him. Why would he need to talk to him about anything?

"Did you happen to hear what they were discussing?"

Max shrugged. "No. Just that it was pretty serious."

"Do you think he would have gone off with Cory to Louisiana to drink and gamble?"

Max yawned again and put his hands behind his head as he stretched out in the office chair. "I would be really surprised to see those two go off on a bender. Talk about opposites. They both have their addictions, but that would just be weird."

Nora pulled out her phone and found Cory's number. She almost never called him, but because they were partners in Brockwell Industries, they were required to stay in touch. Nora put a call through, and after about seven rings, her younger brother answered, his tone groggy and rough. "Hello? Whoever this is, it better be good."

"It's Nora. Have you seen my Uncle Wiley?"

"No." He replied with the sass of a fourteen-year-old. "Why would I have seen him?"

"Because Max said you were talking to him here at the hotel."

"So, what? Not everything is *your* business." The line went dead.

Chapter 19

When Marty came down to work, Nora was on the phone with Lucy. She quietly stowed her purse under the front desk. She was no longer using the cane, but her walk still displayed a slight limp. She straightened the collar of her navy-blue blazer, which was accented with a red scarf and a blue and white striped shirt underneath. Marty had the luxury of a full professional wardrobe after selling real estate for so many years. Lucy had been threatening to take Nora shopping to improve her own wardrobe, but Nora feared she would come home with uncomfortable above-the-knee skirts and four-inch heels.

Lucy's voice could be heard clearly over Nora's phone, even to Marty, who stood a few feet away. "What do you mean he was meeting with Cory?" Lucy said. "What? Did he want to know how to play to an inside straight?"

"I know that sounds crazy. I tried to call Corey, but he told me it was none of my business." Nora sighed, feeling a headache coming on.

"Okay. Let's really look at this. What would Corey have to gain from an association with Wiley?"

That was one of the things Nora liked about Lucy. She had a level head in a crisis. She thought about Lucy's question. There was no connection other than herself.

Lucy continued, "This is tougher than I thought it would be. What do both of these men have in common?"

"Me?"

"Yes, but they don't usually talk about you. They don't have any reason to talk to one another."

Nora absentmindedly tapped her fingers on the desk. "I don't know, but we're back to Moore Foods messing with our orders because their newest employee put an application in to work here." Nora's voice pitched lower. "I'm afraid my uncle has given up sobriety. What am I going to do?"

"Keep calm, big sister. We're not even sure of that yet. Think positive. It's not like he's dead in a ditch somewhere." A wave of guilt washed through Nora. What if he was dead in a ditch? Had she driven him to it?

"Listen, I have a full schedule of appointments this morning, but I could cancel them all and come over. You want me to do that?"

"No. I can handle it. You just got back in town. Just if you hear anything at all from Corey or if you see Wiley, let me know."

"Of course I will. Hang in there. You'll figure it out, and we'll both keep an eye on our brother. I wouldn't trust him for a minute."

"Don't worry about me. So, did you meet any tall, dark, and handsome types in New York City?"

"I'll never kiss and tell, but there were a few interesting men."

"A few? I'm so jealous."

"Oh, you stop. You have Longmire over there. I think you're doing fine in the man department."

Just talking to Lucy seemed to calm her down. After hanging up, she placed a quick call to Moore Foods. "This is Nora over at the Tunie. I was just making sure that our food delivery would be on time today." Nora had decided it was best to call before they were skipped rather than after.

"Yeah, yeah. I know who you are. You're the one who underhandedly tried to steal our distribution gal. You should be ashamed of yourself," the gnarly voice said on the other end.

"I had no idea that Val was going to apply for a job here. It's just that she knew my partner from when she worked here before."

"And she decided to jump ship. Let's see." There was a sound of papers shuffling. "Hmmm. Yes, we will be delivering to the Tunie in the future."

"In the future?"

"You know. We're a very busy wholesaler, but don't worry. You're on the list, somewhere." As Nora ended her call, Marty came out with a fresh batch of brochures for the town sights. She had been so busy on the phone that she hadn't even seen her leave.

As she carefully stacked the brochures on the vertical display shelf, she glanced over and asked, "How are we doing on the food?"

A guest walked by with a t-shirt that said Cats Rule Dogs Drool. Nora started a ferocious sneeze. More residual cat dander.

"That sounds awful," Marty said. "Did you take an antihistamine?"

"Tatty gave me some allergy tea, but I just don't think it's strong enough. I suppose I should take a pill."

"Those teas are for lightweights."

Nora launched into another sneeze when a tall, slender gentleman with blond stubble on his cheek was standing directly behind her. He wore faded skinny jeans, and across the shoulder he sported a leather bag, making him the only man in Piney Woods with a man bag. Nora stepped over to grab a tissue and ran into his broad shoulders.

"I'm sorry. Are you okay?" She teetered slightly to the left, and the man steadied her under her elbow. "Thanks. I didn't see you there. I'm so sorry." Nora looked him over from head to toe. He didn't look like the cat type, but she had to ask. "Are you here for the Meow Meetup?"

"Sort of. I'm here to snoop out the story Alan Shaw was trying to write about. I'm a journalist. Maybe that's where I acquired my silent feet, sneaking up on unsuspecting victims of my next piece."

Nora blew her nose into the tissue and then asked, "Are you Rick?"

"Yes. Are you the person I spoke to on the phone?"

She nodded. "Yes. I'm the owner."

Marty cleared her throat, and Nora corrected herself. "Co-owner of the Tunie. I didn't expect you so quickly. Actually, I'm surprised you came at all."

"Slow news month. I decided to find out how Alan went from reporting the story to being the story. I'm going to need to interview both of you for Alan's murder."

Nora looked around nervously, hoping the Cats Rule T-shirt lady hadn't heard the word murder.

"I hate to have to tell you this, Rick, but we still don't have any rooms," Nora told him.

"Fully booked." Marty confirmed. "We can get you just as soon as the cat people leave."

"Is there any place else I can stay in town?"

"Is Hickelby's booked? That's where Alan Shaw was staying," Marty said.

Nora thought of how she had dumped Alan Shaw at Hickelby's. Things hadn't turned out well for him. Maybe she should be a little nicer to this overflow guest. "How about the Piney Woods B&B?" Having Rick Stephenson stay at the Piney Woods Bed and Breakfast was the least she could do, seeing as he had come a long way for a story.

Marty eyed Nora suspiciously. "That's mighty nice of you to suggest that, Nora. I can call over and check for you if you'd like."

"That would be great. Thanks." Nora turned to Rick. "I can't believe you came to Texas."

"I know. It seems a little spontaneous, but that's the way I am. If I see something I want or get a gut feeling about something, I just go for it."

"You must be hell in the checkout line with all of those impulse items," Nora joked.

Marty broke into the conversation and said, "Nora, they have a room, and Tatty wants you to bring over the list of menu choices Wiley gave you for their anniversary party. She needs to decide today."

Nora had forgotten to bring home the menus after the crazy day she had had yesterday. Even though it wasn't as big as the Meow Meetup, the party would be attended by most of the town and could be a gateway to many more catered affairs from local clientele at the hotel. "Darn. Would you mind if I just ran over there with it? I was supposed to have given it to her days ago and got busy with the convention."

"No problem. I can handle it here. It would be my pleasure after leaving this place to you for so long."

"How about a personal escort, Mr. Stephenson?" Nora said as she grabbed her bag from behind the checkout desk.

"Please, call me Rick," he answered, his low bass rumbling in his chest.

"I'll be back shortly," Nora said as they exited the lobby.

As they began walking down the main street of Piney Woods, Rick Stephenson remarked, "It's not often I get accompanied to my lodgings by such a beautiful redhead. What are you, Irish?"

"You should see my sister." Nora said, smiling.

Chapter 20

During the short walk from the hotel, Nora filled Rick in on some of the town's history. Piney Woods had gone from being an oil boom to an oil bust town, giving it a rags-to-riches to rags reputation. They neared the porch of the Piney Woods Bed and Breakfast to find Ed Tovar up on the stepladder, hanging a bright yellow piece of crepe paper. Even though the anniversary party was going to be at the hotel, Tatty had also opted to decorate the bed and breakfast. The yellow streamers contrasted beautifully with the whites of the gingerbread scroll work on the two-story Victorian home.

Ed shook his head in disgust. "She has me working like a dog, Nora. What's the big deal? It's just an anniversary, right?"

"It is a big deal, and you know it, and you're lucky Tatty didn't hear you say that. I'm just sorry I'm so busy with the hotel right now. The timing of the Meow Meetup convention couldn't have been worse."

Ed took a noble stance. "Don't you worry about us. We'll be fine. We don't mind being ignored by you big hotel tycoon types. We're small potatoes. We get that."

Nora recalled when she left the house that morning that Tatty had knocked herself out for the extra guests that were here for the convention. She had laid out a sumptuous spread of blueberry muffins, scrambled eggs, crisp bacon, and sliced melon. "Do you still have some of the buffet left over?"

"We sure do. Tatty made a bunch of dishes. I could have told her those two skinny city people wouldn't have eaten all that food."

"I'm starved. It sounds great," Rick said, extending his hand.

"I'm Rick Stephenson, and I guess I'll be staying here."

Ed gazed at him suspiciously. "Are you a cat crazy too?"

Rick laughed. "No, no. I knew Alan Shaw. I've come to find out about what happened to him."

Ed leaned closer and lowered his voice. "We'd all like to know that. Are you some kind of cop? Nora hangs out way too much with the fuzz."

"Worse. I'm an investigative reporter."

Ed smiled with excitement as he came down the ladder. "Ah, you are hot on the trail of a story. One thing America can always count on is our media to uncover the true story, or at least their version of it."

"It could be a very big story. I've already been playing with ideas for the headline. Murder in the Piney Woods, or maybe Hotel Homicide," Rick said, causing Nora's blood pressure to rise. What would a headline like that do to the hotel?

"Maybe you could even include the bloody photos taken when your Mr. Shaw lay sprawled on top of the elevator." Ed added.

"Yes sir." He surveyed Ed's work and said, "Your decorations are going to look great."

"Should be. Tatty practically bought out the Dollar Store. You get together with a woman, and then she has to go and celebrate the day she fell for your line over and over again. What a waste of valuable TV time."

"Ed, you've never told us about how you and Tatty met. Was it here in Piney Woods?" Nora asked.

"Oh no. We met at the big daddy of them all. Woodstock in upstate New York. I can remember it like it was yesterday. 1969. We were mixed in with all those kids. We were just kids ourselves."

"How romantic," Nora said with a sparkle in her eye. Rick picked up on her reaction, and a smile spread across his face.

"Oh, yes. We were rocking and rolling with Jimmy Hendricks and Janis Joplin. It was a wonderful time. Very cool."

"You met her there? How did it happen? Did she gaze at you across the crowd of muddy, love-bead wearing hippies?" Rick asked. Nora felt Rick standing very close to her, intently listening to Ed's story. How long would it be until he asked him about the seamier, more sensational side of Woodstock? Who knew what manner of crimes were committed with so many people under the influence? An investigative reporter sees the crime first and humanity second.

"We met there for the first time. She was there with some friends from college. I was there with my buddy Bonzo. It was a wild scene. When I met Tatty, she was trying to deal with some girl who was having a terrible fight with her boyfriend. Tatty was going to drive her home, but I couldn't lose this beautiful girl I had just met. It was like heaven opened up and gave me my Tatty. I tried to convince her to stay. She had those beautiful brown eyes and her laugh. His eyes widened slightly as he spoke of his wife of fifty years. "My God, her laugh was amazing. I knew right then and there I was in love."

"So then, you convinced her not to help that girl?"

"I was sure as hell working on it. I could be pretty persuasive at that age, believe it or not. It ended up not mattering. Her boyfriend came back, and they kissed and made up."

"What was the fight about?" Rick asked.

"He wanted her to do something she didn't want to do. It might've been a festival of free love, but everybody has their rights. If she didn't want to do the Hootchie-Koochie with him in the back of his Volkswagen bus, then she sure didn't have to."

Rick nodded. "That's what the 1960s were all about, anyway. Women were getting their freedom from restrictive societal roles that had been around for decades."

"Yeah, man," Ed said wistfully. "I sure miss those bra burnings."

"Ed. What are you talking about out there?" Tatty said through the open screen door.

"Ugh. Just how beautiful the porch is now that we've added your decorations, my love," Ed answered with a wry smile.

A few minutes later, Tatty had Rick set up with a heaping plate of eggs, bacon, and blueberry muffins. "I'm so glad you came back with the menus and a new boarder. I didn't know what I was going to do with all these leftovers." She spread out her arm, Vanna White style, saying, "I try to serve fresh every day."

Through a mouthful of food, Rick asked, "Ed was telling us how you met at Woodstock."

A knowing look came into Tatty's eyes. "That *viejo loco*. It was a long, long time ago. We ended up here in Piney Woods. Meeting that day was just the beginning. Love goes through many years and phases, you know. I don't even know who those two kids were anymore."

By Tatty's definition Tuck and Nora were just getting to know each other. Everyone at every age has this experience, just in different degrees. Tatty and Ed were in one place, and Nora and Tuck were in another.

Rick gazed at Nora. "You said you had a sister? Is she as beautiful as you are?"

"Even more so. We're a different kind of family. We're sort of ..." Nora stuttered.

"Illegitimate. Born on the wrong side of the sheets," Ed said, once again, the king of tact.

Rick sat back and clapped his hands. "It seems the more questions I ask, the better your story gets, Nora Alexander."

Nora retrieved her phone and pulled up her picture gallery. "Here's a picture of the two of us at a hotel reunion last summer."

Rick looked at the phone, and his eyebrows furrowed as he stared at Nora and her African American sister, two stunningly beautiful women. "Could you possibly be half sisters?"

"You are sharp. We didn't know about each other until we were adults. Our father was one of the town's biggest benefactors."

"Yeah, he spread his love around everywhere," Ed added, stating the obvious.

"Since our father died, we've been in business together. Our brother Cory oversees our father's business, Brockwell Industries."

"Ed Jr. works there," Tatty said. "Brockwell Industries saved Piney Woods from becoming just another dying small town filled with resale shops and antique stores."

Nora nodded. "Yes, and we'll keep Brockwell Industries until we decide to sell it."

"So, you not only have looks that could stop a train, but you're rich? Somebody pinch me."

Nora laughed. "We're not rich. Keep in mind that our income from the warehousing operation is in the hands of a man who has a gambling problem. Not only that, but Corey seems to have had a clandestine meeting with my uncle, who hates him. I wish I knew what was going on there." Nora couldn't believe she had just told a stranger about her family's worries. What was it about him that made her want to tell her innermost secrets? Maybe it was a reporter thing.

Rick pulled a blueberry muffin out of the basket Tatty set on the table. "Okay. So now we have this guy meeting with your uncle. What's the deal with that?"

"My uncle hates Cory. He hated his father, and he feels no differently about his son."

"Your uncle hates your brother. Got it. And has just returned from somewhere for some reason. Hmmm." Rick leaned back as his eyes rose to the ceiling, as if imagining the fate of Corey Brockwell. "If he's been gone a while, have you ever thought he was in some sort of gambling rehab?"

"Gambling rehab? They have a rehab for gamblers." Nora asked.

"Gambling is an addiction, just like anything else. I'm sure there's some sort of twelve-step program for that," Tatty said.

Nora scowled. "Yeah right. Like Corey is ever going to admit he's a prisoner to anything except for the property settlement in our father's will."

"If Adam Brockwell had been alive, he probably would have hired someone to go to rehab for his son." Ed laughed.

"I still want to know why Wiley and Corey would be meeting." Nora asked.

Tatty began to gather up the dishes and carry them to the kitchen. She glanced over at Ed and gave him a nonverbal signal to help her, but he seemed oblivious. "Come on, Ed," Tatty said as she nudged Ed. He jumped as if being woken out of a sound sleep, grunted, and picked up a plate.

Nora sat back and crossed her arms. "I guess worrying about it won't help a thing."

"Nope. Let me get settled in, and then we can have that interview about Alan Shaw's murder. I have a Pulitzer out there with my name on it."

Once again, Nora had to squelch a worry. She glanced at her watch. "I'd better get back."

Chapter 21

When Nora returned to the Tunie, she headed directly to the kitchen. "Have you seen Wiley?"

After such a big breakfast, Rick Stephenson had chosen to stay at the bed and breakfast, get unpacked, and sort through some emails. Caesar, whose face was dusted with flour, turned with a smile.

"He texted me. He says he is on his way. He says he has a new wholesaler for us." There had been a complete transformation in the man. He was no longer pacing and was happily working around the kitchen.

As far as Nora knew, there was only one wholesaler that would deliver to the area, and that was Moore Foods. Had Wiley dropped out of circulation because he drove somewhere out of town to solve the problem?

Dominic spoke up from the front desk. "Nora, there's something wonky with the ice machine on the second floor. Do you think you could go and check that out? Some of the guests were complaining. I need to try to remember to set up my recorders on that floor. It could be poltergeists at work."

"Wonky? Just what does wonky mean?"

"I don't know. What's that got to do with anything? I've been trapped at the front desk, so I couldn't get up there. I figured this was management duty."

Nora shrugged. Why was it that whenever Dominic didn't want to do something, he labeled it management duty? "Sure, I'll look at it." Nora couldn't get Wiley off her mind as she trudged up the stairs to the second-floor ice machine. The old silver-gray dinosaur had come with the Tunie. Hopefully, they wouldn't have to replace it. Just one more outlay of cash they didn't have. If she had to buy a hotel, why didn't she buy a brand-new one? Why did she have to go and buy a hotel that was falling down around her? Nora opened the creaking stairway door onto the second floor and marched over to the ice machine. Just as she rounded the corner from the elevator, she could hear a conversation between a man and a woman.

"It was just so wonderful to see you again. When you told me you were going to be a sheriff in some godless western town, I had no idea it would be this one. You know, I still think of you. Think of those nights in college."

Nora was pretty sure the sulky tones from around the corner were coming from Sasha LeClaire. Her voice practically dripped sexy.

"I was pretty surprised to see you. I mean, you had a cat in college, but weren't you studying fashion design or something?"

"Or something. Cats are where it's at, but enough about me. How about the two of us get together tonight and... relive old times?"

"Um ... I don't know."

Nora recognized the second voice right away. Had Tuck known Sasha in college? From the sounds of their conversation, there was a possibility he knew her very well, and the feeling that was creeping into Nora was not a good one. She cleared her throat and rounded the corner. Sasha was leaning close to Tuck, her finger tracing a line on the seam of his shirt collar. She looked like a cat going in for the kill.

Tuck immediately jumped back, pulling Sasha's hand away. "Nora."

"That's my name. Really glad you haven't forgotten it yet."

A mischievous look came into Sasha's eyes. "Am I to assume that the two of you are some kind of backcountry item? Where did you meet? The watermelon seed-spitting contest?"

"Sasha." Tuck scolded, and then his tone changed as he turned toward Nora, whose flushed face betrayed her anger. "This is my girlfriend, Nora Alexander."

"I knew you did a lot around here, but I had no idea you were Tuck's latest." The words sounded complimentary, but the look in her deep brown eyes displayed something else. Something that made Nora feel small. She didn't need this, so she started to push past them.

"I have work to do."

"Oh, rooms to clean?" Once again, Sasha had deflated what she had left of her dignity.

"No, actually. I have to ..." Nora's chin rose. "Fix the ice machine."

Sasha stifled a giggle with a well-manicured hand.

"Nora," Tuck called after her. "We'll talk about this tonight."

"Sure," Nora answered.

As if to add to her humiliation, the carpet she crossed to the ice machine slurped with every step. Opening the closet door, she pulled out a mop and bucket. She would have to grab the shopvac from downstairs to finish the job. If she didn't get on it now, the carpet would begin to stink with mold. Nora began to mop up the residue and then checked behind the ice machine. Assessing the problem, she immediately knew they would not have to buy a new ice machine anytime soon.

Most of these things worked much better when you kept them plugged in. After she returned the plug to the socket, the ice machine responded with a soft whir as it began to fill with water. She would have to remember to tell Dominic that his poltergeist had unplugged the ice machine.

As she straightened up, Tuck had moved to stand directly behind her. "Really, Nora, it isn't what it looks like. And as long as we're on the subject, what about you and this reporter?"

Tuck tried to say something else, but he was interrupted when his phone went off. He read the screen and then looked up. "I have to get this. I have to head off to Lubbock for a meeting, but save me some time tonight, and we'll talk about this." Nora slammed the mop into the bucket, hearing Sasha's laughter behind her.

Nora stomped down the stairs, hoping that the sounds of her footfalls would be louder than the sobs that were now coming out of her. How could he do this to her? She stopped at the door to the lobby on the main floor, wiped her eyes, ran her fingers through her hair, and stood tall. When she entered the lobby, Camille Martin-Ortega was standing at the check-in desk. Dominic, upon spotting her, motioned her over.

"Thank goodness you're back. Miss Ortega is here..."

"Martin-Ortega," the woman snapped.

Dominic cleared his throat and tried it again. "Yeah. Right. Ms. Martin-Ortega said she discussed a discount for the convention guests with you."

Just what Nora needed right now. "We discussed it, but we didn't settle it." Nora's tone was abrupt and all business.

The Meow Meetup organizer held up a small tablet. On the screen was Alan Shaw's article slamming the Tunie. "I believe this is all I need to solidify our agreement. Lucky for you, most of our guests still haven't seen this, but you can bet they will be reading it shortly. I plan to print out this article and include it with their exit packets. You can also bet that we will never be returning to your hotel."

Still rolling off the anger brewing inside of her from catching Tuck, there was no way she was letting this woman cheat her out of the original booking price. She had worked too hard to set up this convention, and there was no way she was giving into this petty two-named woman. "Fine. I don't think we would enter into negotiations with you for your next convention, anyway. As for a discount, I still need to discuss that with my partner."

"Take all the time you want, as long as it's by this afternoon. I will be busy all day with the arrival of our show cat, Catpurnicus, anyway. You did bring in the extras we requested? The fresh-caught tuna, the scratching post, and the calming lavender?"

This "show cat" required more attention than a rock star prima donna. "Yes. Our staff is ready for Catpurnicus."

"Good. The owner is picking him up at the local kennel right now. I do not understand why a cat of this stature can't just stay here at the hotel, but now I'm sure that a true four-star hotel would have handled this much more efficiently." Ms. Martin-Ortega fastened the covering over her tablet with a short snap and slipped it back into her bag.

After the Meow Meetup organizer left, Nora threw her hands in the air and let out a rumbling sound. "If it isn't one thing, it's another. When will things start going right around here?"

Dominic stepped back slightly, his eyebrows raised. "Would you like to go on break? I mean, I know you just got here, sugar, but maybe a break would be good for you right now."

"I don't need a break. I just got back from breakfast."

"Okay. I think you do. There are negative forces at work in you. Maybe I should run the thermal camera to see if you have any cold spots or a negative entity. Did you go somewhere where you might have picked up something? You know I have my suspicions about that ballroom."

"We call it the banquet room now, and anyway, I wasn't here. I dropped a guest over at Tatty and Ed's. An investigative reporter is here to check out what happened to Alan Shaw."

"Really? I love watching those guys on TV. How does Tuck feel about you moving a TV personality into your home?"

"I never said he was on TV, and I don't give a damn what Tuck likes."

"What happened?" Dominic lowered his voice so as not to inform the entire lobby full of guests that Nora was angry with her boyfriend.

"I went upstairs to fix the ice machine, and guess who I ran into talking about old times with a former girlfriend? Tuck and that Uber sexy woman with the cat website."

Dominic's deep brown eyes widened. "Tuck? Damn. Talk about getting busted. She was va-va-va-voom, baby."

"He said it was all a misunderstanding, and it wasn't what it looked like."

"What else could it have been? She's something else, if you know what I mean. Your man was definitely catting around."

"My thoughts exactly," Nora said, feeling the anger inside of her moving over for pure old-fashioned sadness.

Dominic moved closer and slipped an arm around her shoulders. "Ah, come on, kid. Now I've upset you. I have never pretended to know anything about the affairs of the heart, but could it be he was telling the truth?"

"I wish I could believe that."

"I see. Where is he now? You need me to go straighten him out?" Dominic pounded one fist into the other.

"No. Thanks though."

"Then why don't you go and ask him to tell you what was really going on? Give him the benefit of the doubt. We fellas can be dense in the head sometimes. Maybe she is just an old girlfriend who thought she could bat those gorgeous eyes and that he should naturally come running. A woman like that doesn't know the meaning of rejection. I think my track record speaks for itself on that issue."

"I can't. He's driving over to Lubbock for a meeting. He won't be back until late tonight."

"Maybe it's all just a misunderstanding. Trust me. Being a man of the world, I've learned that sometimes you have to assess the situation more than once."

"I don't know. I don't exactly have a good record with men. All the men in my life have either left or screwed me over. It makes me want to join a convent."

"There is no need to go that far. You ain't no Sister of Mercy. Besides, who does that these days?" Dominic said it with a smile.

"I guess you're right."

"Just trust old Dom here. This will work itself out. You'll be mooning over that cop in no time."

Chapter 22

When Rick Stephenson walked in a few minutes later, Nora's head was still spinning from what she had witnessed on the second floor. Was it all an innocent mistake? Would she ever trust him again? Rick started talking, oblivious to the emotion boiling up inside of her.

"So now that I moved in to the bed and breakfast, let's get down to business. What exactly do you know about Alan's doings? Can you take me to the crime scene? Did he ask you any pointed questions about Evangeline Cartwright, this mystery writer?"

Nora's gaze was slightly off center. Of all the men out there, she never would've suspected that Tuck would ever be involved with a woman who used that much eyeliner.

"Nora? Are you listening?"

Dominic leaned over the counter. "You'll have to excuse her. Someone just broke her heart. Stories like hers will haunt this hotel forever."

Rick looked at Nora again and lowered his voice. "I'm so sorry. But now that I have your attention, is there any chance you have any photos from the crime scene before they cleaned it up?"

Nora looked around. The lobby was now empty due to the preparations going on in the banquet room for the great show cat, Catpurnicus. "Okay, let's talk about why you came here. First off, I would really appreciate it if you would not mention the word murder.

We are trying to run a business here that is based on people feeling at home on the road."

"Are you serious? You want to cover this up?" Rick dug in his heels. "I've cracked coverups bigger than this one, and now that a fellow newsman has been murdered, you can bet I'm going to blow this investigation wide open."

Nora pulled Rick in closer. "As far as Alan Shaw goes, I did have possession of his laptop, but the police took it as evidence."

Dominic leaned into the pair and said, "That would be the aforementioned boyfriend."

"Great."

"There is not much you can do on that front." Nora didn't tell Rick about Tuck's investigation of the laptop, which came up with nothing. She had the feeling that the more she told Rick about anything, the more she would regret it.

"Alan was a pretty paranoid guy. Like I told you before, he was a big conspiracy theory nut. He might park his stuff on the cloud. I'll have to check what he was storing at the office. Where is his luggage? Did the police get that too?"

"Yes." Nora liked the way that Rick was thinking systematically while working through the problem. She only wished he had been around when she was trying to get rid of the one-star reviews. "We think Mr. Shaw might have been responsible for leaving a slew of bad reviews about the hotel. He was angry because, like you, he couldn't rent a room."

Rick smirked. "Why does that not shock me? Alan had a way of worming his way into a situation. You wouldn't be the first hotel clerk who wished she had never met the man."

Doug Lindstrom walked in, accompanied by a lady with pink streaks in her hair who was carrying a cat carrier. This had to be the arrival of the great Catpurnicus.

"If you'll excuse me for just a moment," Nora said to Rick.

"Oh. No worries. I'm going to the fourth floor to look for damage from the mur... incident."

Nora stepped over to Doug and the cat owner. "Is this our guest of honor?"

"It certainly is. I'm Mitzy Olson, his owner," the woman answered, her voice a nasal ring that reminded Nora of a squeaky door. "Perny is a little parched. Do you have any Perrier?"

The cat owner dropped the "r" in the word parched, making it come out as "poched." Nora turned to Dominic. "See if we have any Perrier in the kitchen."

Dominic nodded and hustled toward the dining room.

Doug leaned close to Nora's ear. "Please take this woman. She's driving us all crazy out at the kennel."

Nora put on her best hospitality smile and whisked Catpurnicus and his owner to the banquet room. It was just downright cruel to make a dog lover cater to a celebrity cat.

When Nora entered the banquet room, they were trying to get Catpurnicus settled in a soft black velvet bed in front of a display of red and blue ribbons and various trophies.

Catpurnicus was sturdy-looking. Nothing like the thin Siamese cats Nora would expect to see as a best-in-show winner. Dominic approached the boxy red hair with an assortment of tuna on a silver platter. Catpurnicus sniffed at it, put out an evil-sounding growl at Dominic, and turned away.

"That'll never do," squeaked the picky cat's owner. "Is that bluefin tuna from the Atlantic? Don't you dare try to parade any of that Pacific Albacore in here. This is a champion cat. Perhaps I should have offered it to him. He is not an outwardly social animal. He is very careful about who he chooses to befriend. Like his tuna, he associates with only the best of humans."

Nora knew the tuna was exactly what they had ordered because she was the one who had to track it down. If the cat didn't like the tuna, then it wasn't from a lack of trying on her end.

Doug Lindstrom smirked in the corner. Nora couldn't imagine all that this little woman had demanded for Catpurnicus already. The prized feline escaped from its velvet throne and headed for the open kitchen passageway. If Mr. Janson from the health department were to step in unannounced, he would shut the Tunie down for sure. Nora quickened her step to head it off before he did any damage to the kitchen.

When Nora entered the kitchen, she found her uncle Wiley bent on one knee, feeding the cat a bite of the fried chicken he had prepared for the guests. Catpurnicus, who had looked regal and off-putting in the dining room, now purred against her uncle's leg.

"That's a good little kitty. Did one of these kitty ladies sneak you in?" His voice bordered on baby talk, making Nora smile. His owner was right. Catpurnicus only associates with the best humans.

"That's our headliner this afternoon," Nora said.

"Oh? This is the big cat act they were all talking about? It can't be right. It just seems like a cat to me."

From behind Nora, the cat's owner cleared her throat. "Not just any cat. Three-time grand champion of this nation's cat shows. Oh, my God. What are you feeding him?"

"Fried chicken."

Nora thought the lady would swoon and fall on the kitchen floor in a pink huff.

"It's okay. He likes it." Wiley picked up the cat and petted it. Nora motioned to him to follow her to the banquet room, where Wiley returned Catpurnicus to his throne. Camille Martin-Ortega then took over again, and Nora joined Doug Lindstrom, who had been observing the entire scene as he leaned his lanky frame against the conference room wall.

"Well played, there, Nora."

"You do what you have to do."

"Isn't that the truth?" he answered, the mirth showing in his smile.

Chapter 23

After saying goodbye to Doug, who was joining Catpurnicas in the banquet room, Nora returned to the front desk, where Max and Dominic were waiting for her. "Nora, if you're back from dealing with cat royalty, Marty would like to speak with you."

"Um, tell her I'll be with her in just a minute."

Max's eyebrows rose. "Sure boss. Whatever you say. Oh, and there is some kind of reporter dude wandering around. Do you know anything about that?" Nora had forgotten about Rick Stephenson. If he had interviewed any of the guests to ask about Alan Shaw's murder, it would be just one more thing to dump on Marty.

"Is Marty in the office?"

"Yep."

"Don't you even know it's payday?" Dominic asked. "Or do owners not take a salary?"

He didn't know how close to the truth he was, Nora thought. Rick Stephenson came out of the elevator, but before he stepped out, he ran his hand along the wood molding around the opening. "He had to have struggled. The frame upstairs is broken in several places," Rick said, seemingly to nobody. Nora rushed over in an effort to squelch him once again.

"Why don't you come into the office, and you can tell me your findings?"

His eyes took Nora in. "Sure. I need to use your computer anyway." He gazed over at the business center. "No offense, but those computers look pretty old." Once again, a member of the press had insulted her computer. Nora didn't even know why she had decided to set them up. No one seemed to need them, and the people who did couldn't stand them.

When Nora and the reporter entered the business office, Marty was hunched over the keyboard with the bookkeeping software pulled up. She smiled at Nora. "I know you usually do this, but you've been so busy with the convention, I thought I would try to print out the checks." The bookkeeping software was Nora's baby, and Marty had never ventured into it before.

"Dominic reminded me it was payday. I should have taken care of it before the convention started. Next time, I'll schedule better. If you'll let me get at the computer, I'll be happy to print out the checks."

"And she also needs to let me work on it," Rick added.

Marty's eyes took in the tall man. "Are you an accountant?"

"No. A reporter. I just need to look up some information on Alan Shaw. If I'm going to write about his murder, I need some background information." A panic shot through Marty's expression, revealing she felt the same as Nora had. Publicity about a murder could ruin their business.

"You didn't bring a computer?"

"I did, but it's at the bed and breakfast. My bad," Rick answered.

"Well, then. Why don't you go back there and do your work?" Marty suggested.

Rick's eyes narrowed. "You wouldn't be trying to limit the free press, would you?"

"I'm a tremendous believer in free press as well as self-preservation. What happened here was a terrible accident. I'm sure there are many more salacious stories you could be working on."

"No. I have already told your partner that covering up this story will only make it worse. Don't you know that with every coverup, a conspiracy theorist is born?"

Nora now felt bad for bringing Rick into the business office. She wished she had never called First Reporter, but she had been desperate to get control of the one-star reviews.

"Fine. If you won't let me use the computer, then you can at least answer a couple of questions. Do you have any idea who might have murdered Alan Shaw?"

Marty shrugged. "I didn't know the man. I never even met him until the day he was taken away."

"I see."

"Me either," Nora added. "He came into the hotel, caused a lot of fuss with Evangeline Cartwright, and then he was dead."

Rick stroked his chin. "You said that before. Do you think I could interview this Evangeline Cartwright?"

"All I can do is ask. She will probably be glad to talk to you. She is a very nice lady."

Marty scowled. "Especially to reporters."

Nora turned Rick to the door. "Why don't you go back to the bed and breakfast and do your research? I'll see if I can find Evangeline and set up the interview."

Rick nodded. "I suppose. It is still a puzzle to me how Alan could set foot in a town this small and get himself murdered."

"Welcome to Texas."

Chapter 24

As soon as Rick closed the door, Max's voice came over the office intercom.

"Uh, Marty. We have a slight problem."

Marty had come in to do the paychecks, but instead was met with a second interruption.

"What?"

"Uh, just come out here. If Nora is there, we'll need her too."

"On our way," Marty said as she pressed the intercom button.

"Guess paychecks will be a little late," Nora said.

As Nora and Marty walked toward the front desk, Evangeline and Doug were heading into the restaurant. Max nearly ran into them as he moved his large frame toward Marty and Nora. "If you are through giving information to that reporter about how Alan Shaw died, we have a gigantic problem."

Evangeline drew closer. "Oh my, poor Mr. Shaw. Such a terrible accident. I'm a little surprised the press would be interested."

"We're all a little unnerved by it," Nora said. "The reporter also asked if he could speak with you. You were Mr. Shaw's last interview subject after all."

Evangeline's hand went to her throat, and her face reddened. "Really? I find that quite surprising. There's not much I can tell the man, but I suppose I could meet with him."

"Good. He's staying at the Piney Woods B&B."

Max interrupted, "Listen, folks, I know this is all really interesting, but we have a bigger problem."

Marty turned to Max. "So, what is the problem? The hotel isn't on fire, so this better be good." Marty said.

Doug spoke next. "Catpurnicus. He escaped, and no one can find him. We've all been searching for the last ten minutes."

"What? Are you kidding me?" Nora asked, her head spinning. She walked over to the banquet room, which was now almost completely empty except for one woman calling in a high-pitched voice. "Here, Kitty, Kitty."

"Do you think he might have gotten outside?" Nora asked.

Doug nodded. "That is our main concern. Most of the convention goers have spread out and are searching street by street."

Marty nodded, taking the information in. "Thank goodness Piney Woods is not that big. Just another good thing about living in a small town."

"And you've searched the hotel?" Nora asked.

Max sighed. "Yes."

Nora sat down on a red bench against the wall. "This can't be happening."

"Yes, well, at least the first day went off without a hitch," Max said, and then was interrupted by Nora.

"We had a murder on the first day."

Evangeline's eyes widened. "Murder? I thought it was an accident."

Nora straightened up. "Yes, of course. An accident."

Neither Evangeline nor Doug looked convinced. The truth was about to come out, and Nora knew she couldn't cover it up for much longer. Rick was right. There was a conspiracy theorist out there, just waiting to be born.

"Well, my dear. Shall we join the search?" Doug offered an arm to Evangeline.

"Why not?" Evangeline fairly twinkled back. The chemistry between them was almost overwhelming.

After they left, Marty sat next to Nora. "Listen, kid, quit beating yourself up. I messed up my ankle, and even if I had wanted to walk on it, Max wouldn't let me. I'm just glad you were there to cover for both of us. Do you know how awesome that is? You couldn't have predicted Mr. Shaw would get pushed down the elevator shaft, and you couldn't have predicted that a pampered feline would run off."

The guilt was seeping into Nora like a wine stain on a white silk blouse. "Marty. I appreciate all the faith that you had in me, but I haven't quite told you everything."

"What?"

"Ms. Martin-Ortega wants a 50 percent discount because of the one-star reviews that she found on the computer left by Alan Shaw."

"Our dead guy?"

"The dead guy. He left the reviews before somebody did him in."

"I got that part," Marty informed her.

"Then he went on to write a magazine article that I'm still trying to get retracted."

"Wow, it's amazing how quickly she found out." Marty said.

"Correct."

"I can deal with Mrs. Martin-Ortega. Even though we have some ridiculous reviews out there, it is not true, and we have delivered the services that they ordered. It wouldn't stand up in court, so she can put her justified outrage to bed."

Nora had to admit that she admired how Marty was not at all bothered by the situation. She had known all along that the discount was not a fair shake for them, but she didn't have the presence of mind to do what Marty very easily decided.

"Why didn't you tell me all of this was going on?"

"I don't know." Nora sounded like a guilty child.

"Has Tuck shared anything with you about his investigation?"

"I'm not too happy with your nephew right now."

Marty's eyes widened. "Did you have a fight?"

"Has he ever mentioned an old girlfriend from college named Sasha?"

Marty put both hands over her mouth in amazement. "Sasha? Let me think." She bit her bottom lip. "He's got the family looks, so you have to know he had several girlfriends during college."

"Sasha LeClaire was one of them and is ready to pick up where they left off. I caught her trying to snuggle up to him in the hallway."

The lobby door opened, and Val smiled when she saw Marty. "Marty! I don't know if you've heard it or not, but I'm officially fired with bad references from Moore Foods. Please tell me you have an opening here. Did you look at my application yet?"

"Not yet, but heard about it," Marty answered, and then looked to Nora.

"You're hired," Nora said, surprising herself.

Val jumped. "I am?" She turned to Val and repeated her question. "I am? That's great. I promise you will not be sorry. Besides that, when I quit over at Moore Foods, I left a bunch of nasty reviews on the business rating site. What they did to you guys is bordering on illegal. I'll tell you, those guys are like the food mafia. There is nothing I'd put past them."

Marty ran over and put an arm around her old friend.

"When can you start?"

"As soon as you need me. I just know there are so many things you can make better around here. It will be just like the old days. This is so exciting."

Marty and Val walked away from her arm in arm. After Marty's kind words just a few moments ago, she knew she could handle Val's presence a little better now. If nothing else, it would give her more time to deal with the boatload of trouble she seemed to be constantly working through. Yes, having Val around was a good thing.

Chapter 25

Nora returned to the conference room to see if there had been any updates on Catpurnicus, the runaway cat.

Camille Martin-Ortega held a pink-bling-encrusted cell phone to her ear as she stood there, engrossed in conversation. "I think we need an APB or whatever it is you police people do. This cat is worth thousands of dollars. No, sir, this is not stolen property. It's a cat." With a punch of a manicured fingernail, she hung up on whatever poor soul she had tangled with at the police department.

"No luck?" Nora asked.

Camille's eyes narrowed. "Do I look like I have the world's most famous cat back in its cage? No luck." She then began to mutter to herself. "I should have hired security. I should have booked a hotel that provided security, massages, and a free bar."

Marty entered the conference room and was clearly still excited that they had hired Val. "Isn't it great? I just left Val with Wiley. She's trying to get to know the place all over again. She knows Wiley from the old days, and they're talking about ways to promote the restaurant." A little late to the party, she took in the mood of the room. "Everyone is still out looking for that cat."

"Yes," Nora answered before Camille could add any other negativity to the situation.

Doug Lindstrom entered, his eyes searching the room. "They sent me after the cat carrier."

This was good news. This could be the end of the exhausting search and a chance for the convention guests to return to the hotel. "Have they found him? Is he okay?"

"Don't know. They just wanted to be able to crate him if they did find him," Doug answered.

Marty shook her head in disbelief. "That's too bad. I'm surprised the owner would ever take her eyes off an animal that valuable."

"At least we can keep this quiet, hopefully. Thank God, there are no reporters left to cover the conference," Camille said.

Nora bit her lip, trying to find a way to break this to the convention organizer gently. "Actually, there is a reporter here. After the first one was ... died, a second one showed up."

"Just like cockroaches," Marty added.

"Are you kidding me?" Doug sounded tired. "I'm curious how the second reporter even found out about Mr. Shaw."

"I was trying to do some research on Alan Shaw to find out what magazine he had been working for. I found one magazine he submitted to regularly and called them. That was when I spoke to a reporter named Rick Stephenson. He knew Alan and flew here on the trail of a story."

"Are my ears burning?" Rick Stephenson stepped into the conference room. "I was going to try to interview that mystery writer, but it seems the hotel is empty."

"We have a missing grand champion cat on the loose," Camille said, her haughty manner immediately putting him in his place.

"Sorry to hear about that. So, when is this cat search going to be over? I have some pretty interesting theories on Alan Shaw's death, and I want to interview this hotel full of suspects before they all head back home."

Doug stepped forward and asked, "Why do you want to interview Evangeline?"

"And you are?" Rick asked.

Doug cleared his throat. "A friend."

"Okay, friend," Rick said. "I always like to start at the beginning, where the victim was."

Marty quickly answered, as if one statement could make his investigation finished. "Alan Shaw fell down the elevator shaft. It's a terrible thing, but hardly worth an investigative report."

Camille cocked her head to the side. "Can we even be sure that Mr. Shaw fell? What if he was pushed?"

Marty switched at the air with her hand as if pushing away Camille Martin-Ortega's theory. "Murder? Murder at the Tunie? I don't think so."

"Yes, well, we can talk about this thing, or I can go out and investigate it. I think I'll just walk around and see who I can interview." Rick gave a halfhearted wave and, with long strides, left the conference room.

Doug lifted the cat carrier. "I'd better get going. I'd hate to be responsible for missing the rescue of His Highness Catpurnicus." Doug nodded and stepped back out into the lobby.

"We should go, too," Marty said. "Let's not leave Dominic at the front desk for too long. He'll be teaching Val how to set up ghost traps."

"Excuse me?" Camille asked. "Am I to understand you have ghosts here too?" Her phone began to ring.

Nora squeezed her shoulder. "Of course not!"

As they made a quick exit to the front desk, Dominic was busy telling a story to a distracted guest. Marty whispered to Nora. "I'm sorry for mentioning Dominic and his ghost traps. Here I am back at work, and I'm already causing problems. You really have been someone I could rely on during this time. You were so consistent and professional about everything that I felt like the hotel was running smoothly. I really appreciate that."

Marty's words were so kind that Nora knew she needed to be honest with her partner. "Marty, I need to tell you something."

"What?" From the look on Marty's face, she didn't have any idea of Nora's deceptiveness. "I might have purposely hidden Val's application."

"Why?"

"It sounds silly now, but maybe I was a little jealous."

Marty stopped and turned to Nora. "Are you serious?"

Nora looked at the carpet and didn't answer.

"I have news for you, red," Marty said. "No one could replace you."

"Thanks."

"You have set up a wonderful conference. The first conference in the history of our partnership."

"What about Ms. Martin-Ortega's insistence on a discount based on the fake reviews? Do you think we should even consider it?"

"Why would we do that? A review is simply an opinion that can be factually inaccurate, a point proven by Mr. Shaw's reviews."

"I know. I totally agree with you on that."

"Good. Besides that, you had them all retracted."

Nora sighed. "Then he went on to write a magazine article that I'm still trying to get retracted."

"That little weasel spent a lot of time tearing us down. People like that should be arrested."

"I just have to wonder if he made somebody angry enough to push him down an elevator shaft." Nora said, reasserting her theory of murder.

"Now, if you are finished with all this confession business, let's go check on Val."

"Yes let's. I need to talk to Uncle Wiley anyway."

Nora had to find out what he had been up to and why Wiley had left Cesar with so much responsibility. When she and Marty entered the bustling kitchen, Wiley was looking into the walk-in freezer. Val was busy writing something down on a pad of paper.

"Uncle Wiley, may I speak to you for a moment?" Nora asked.

Wiley led her to the rear of the kitchen and turned to her. "I figured you'd be coming in here when you got the time." He rubbed the back of his neck gingerly.

"You figured right," Nora said. "Word is that you were huddled together with none other than my unreliable half brother last night. Then you mysteriously disappeared. I don't know which part of that alarms me more. Are you making plans with Corey, or are you possibly returning to your old ways?"

Wiley held up a bony hand. "I'll be the first to admit that this whole convention thing has made me want to take a drink or two, but God willing, I haven't done it yet. I think the worst is probably over for us."

"Meaning what? How can the worst be over? We still don't have a reliable supplier. Moore Foods didn't think twice about firing Val."

"I heard that. When I used to work for Jumbo Jim, Moore Foods was Johnny on the Spot. Now that I'm working for their competition, I'm like a bad first date. No calls, no letters. But not to worry, Nora dear, I've got it under control."

There was a knock on the door that opened to the alley. "Excuse me, I have a delivery for Wiley McArdle."

Wiley's chest puffed up. "That's me. I'm Wiley. Bring it on over here."

The man rolled four boxes on a dolly over to Wiley. He handed him a shipping list. Wiley looked through it carefully. "Aha. It looks like everything's here. I'll sign for it. Excellent work, my man."

The man in his crisp sky-blue uniform wasn't from Moore Foods. She walked around the box to see the logo. Brockwell Industries was printed on the side. Uncle Wiley was ordering food through the warehousing operation of Brockwell Industries. Didn't he understand how dishonest Corey Brockwell could be? Even though Nora was a young woman, she felt the flush of rising blood pressure.

Wiley cockily crossed his arms as he grinned at the driver. He had solved the Tunie's delivery problem, but did he have to consort with the devil to do it? "You can just put those boxes over there. Any more?"

The driver tipped his hat. "That's all for today, sir."

"Thanks so much. I'll be sure to tell your boss what an outstanding job you're doing."

As soon as the driver left, Nora tore into Wiley. "Are you kidding me?"

Before Wiley could answer, Marty and Val walked in. Marty was giving Val the fifty-cent tour. "And check out the improvements we've made in the kitchen for the hotel. We don't want to brag, but our little restaurant has become one of the hot spots in Piney Woods."

Val looked around at the shiny stainless-steel counters and the busy employees of the kitchen. "Is it always this hot in here?"

"Just wait until we really start cooking," Wiley answered with a gleam in his eye. He might be getting up there, but he still had a little flirt in him.

Marty's eyes fell on the boxes in the corner. "Excellent Nora. Did you get it straightened out with Moore Foods?"

Before Nora could answer, Val answered for her. "Those boxes are not from Moore."

"Which is just what we were about to discuss, Marty. Wiley here has decided to take it upon himself to go into business with Brockwell Industries. This came from the big warehouse. I didn't even know that they had wholesale food orders over there."

Wiley held up a hand to stop Nora before she launched into another speech about going behind her back. "Up to now, they haven't. I spoke with Corey last night about the monopoly our food wholesaler had in Piney Woods and how they could decide the fate of a restaurant. He agreed it was unfair and had food shipped in overnight. He's setting it up so that we get all the food through him. And it's cheaper to boot."

Val clapped her hands together in excitement. "What an excellent idea, Wiley. Man, will they be angry over at Moore Foods. Jumbo Jim just lost his stranglehold over you guys and his reason to slip them a little extra to put the screws to you."

"Good job, Wiley," Marty added.

Nora couldn't believe what she was hearing. Didn't anybody else in this kitchen realize what a terrible idea it was to go into business with Corey Brockwell? She had spent the better part of the last six months avoiding the man, and now they would cross paths every week in the form of boxes full of food. "We can't accept this food."

"Why not?" Val asked. "Wiley has figured out a way around the poor treatment you've been receiving. I think it's just short of genius."

"Because this food comes from Corey Brockwell. No good will come of it. Every time I've had anything to do with this man, it's turned out badly."

"Corey's Nora's brother," Wiley explained.

Val opened her mouth in surprise. "Corey Brockwell is your brother? I didn't know Mr. Brockwell and his wife had another child."

"They didn't."

Val's eyes widened in surprise.

Marty stepped forward with her arms folded. "Nora, I know you have problems with Corey, but this is not a personal or emotional decision. This is a business, and in business, sometimes you have to work with people you don't necessarily like. Wiley made the decision, and frankly, our problem is solved. End of discussion."

Wiley nodded and beamed at Val. She had another convert by her side and hadn't even tried. Nora threw her hands up in the air and walked out of the kitchen. The decision to acquire a new wholesaler had been made, and she had very little control over it.

Chapter 26

Nora was still angry later that evening when she sat down to dinner with Evangeline Cartwright and Doug Lindstrom. Max had come up with the ingenious idea of showing the movie version of the Broadway play *Cats*, and most of the convention crowd was in the banquet room watching the musical.

"So, no luck in finding Mr. Catpurnicus?" Nora asked.

Doug sighed, "No, sadly. We all split up and searched the entire town. I think he caught the Greyhound bus to Dallas."

Evangeline smiled. "So sad, really. His owner is beside herself. It just goes to show you the value some people put in their animals."

"The stud fee for an animal like that is at least $1500 a pop, my dear. Catpurnicus is not just a beloved pet but an income stream for that woman," Doug said.

Caesar came to the table with three fresh green salads. "Where is Mr. Tuck tonight?"

"He should be on his way back from Lubbock," Nora said flatly, unrolling her napkin and placing it on her lap. She was starting to feel like he might have truly been an innocent victim of Sasha LeClaire's advances. At least she hoped that was the case.

"Of course, Miss Nora. Of course." He quickly took their orders and exited the dining room.

"So much has happened in the last few days. We have a dead reporter, a missing grand champion cat, and now a second reporter. Whoever said small towns were boring?" Evangeline joked.

"Speaking of a second reporter," Doug said to Evangeline. "Are you prepared for that?"

"I have to be honest with you. All of this just makes me uncomfortable."

Nora picked at her salad and said, "I'm surprised he isn't here tonight. He was pretty hot on the trail. Now that it's just us, I need to share something. He thinks Alan Shaw was murdered."

Evangeline gasped. "What would lead him to such a conclusion? I thought it was an accident."

"There is obvious breakage in the wood around the elevator. I wouldn't want this to get around, but the police think it was murder," Nora said. Evangeline seemed to grow rigid the more they discussed Alan Shaw's death.

"What about that little librarian woman?" Doug asked. "Is she being questioned?"

"Yes, she is one of the suspects."

Caesar came out and picked up the salad plates to replace them with their meals. They continued their conversation as soon as he was out of earshot. "She's the only one in town with any kind of motive. No one else even knew the guy. I think she might be one of those nutty super fans."

"I can't believe that," Evangeline said. "My fans are usually genuinely nice people. It's the thriller writers who get all the wackos."

Nora scratched her temple. Someone who was premeditating murder would want to have a method that was foolproof. Alan Shaw could have survived that fall long enough to be rescued. If the hotel hadn't been empty before the convention guests arrived, he might've survived and been able to tell the world who pushed him.

Nora's sister Lucy walked into the dining room, looked around, and headed directly for their table. Nora was surprised to see her. "Lucy? What are you doing here?"

"Just trying to track you down and make sure you haven't got yourself stuck in anymore elevators, sis."

Nora stood and placed an arm around Lucy. "This is my sister Lucy. Lucy, this is Doug Lindstrom and our guest of honor, Evangeline Cartwright." Even though Lucy and Nora were sisters, their physical appearance couldn't be any more different.

"And you say you are sisters?" Evangeline asked. "Adoption?"

Lucy smiled. "It's a long story."

"Won't you join us for dinner?" Doug asked.

Lucy glanced at her watch and then said, "What the heck? Mom isn't expecting me for an hour, anyway."

Doug reached over to another table and grabbed a chair. Lucy graciously accepted it. Another waiter came out of the kitchen holding a plate and silverware. He set it in front of Lucy and rearranged the other plates on the table.

"Thank you. What happened to Caesar?" Nora asked.

"He said he's been here for twelve long hours. So, he had to go home."

After the waiter finished with the place setting, Lucy touched Nora on the arm. "You look like you're still in one piece after being trapped in the elevator. It's just awful what happened. You're lucky you didn't fall down that big hole yourself. Where's Tuck? Shouldn't he be here swooning over you?"

"He's busy, but he's stopping by tomorrow. So much has happened that it's hard to remember. My elevator mishap happened the day before Alan Shaw ended up at the bottom of the shaft."

The waiter brought over a basket of bread, and Lucy immediately grabbed a piece. "I haven't eaten since breakfast. There does seem to be a lot going on around the elevator. I hate to be the first to say it, but what if Alan Shaw was pushed?"

"We were just discussing that possibility," Evangeline said. "You know, as a mystery writer, I should be all over this. Somehow, though, it's different when it happens in real life. Where are all those quirky characters and near-genius amateur sleuths?"

Doug buttered a piece of bread. "Who would think working in a hotel would be so dangerous?"

"You're telling me," Nora said.

Doug's eyes rolled over Lucy. "And what is it that you do? Are you also in the hotel business?"

"No. I'm a financial planner. I help people make money." Lucy had a twinkle in her eye as she flashed a smile.

They enjoyed their dinner, and Evangeline filled them in on what it was like to be a writer. It seemed so different from working in a hotel and required a lot of time working alone. Nora wasn't sure she could ever be motivated to work all by herself, day after day. Then again, after all the crazy things that were happening during this convention, a little peace and quiet sounded very attractive to her. As Evangeline spoke, Nora couldn't help but notice the admiration in Doug's eyes.

He was in love with her.

"I'd better be going. I promised Mama I'd stop by on the way home to tell her about the accident. She picked up an evening shift." Lucy's mother continued to work at Shady Sunsets even though her daughter had come into an inheritance. When asked about it, she stated she had always looked after herself and wasn't going to start mooching on her daughter.

"Besides, that's where my friends are now. I might as well be there for them," Arnette Cooper had told Lucy.

"Lord knows why she's working so many hours. It's not like she needs the money," Lucy said as she put back on her heels that she had kicked off under the table. Lucy looped her arm through Nora's. "I want you to know that if you need anything, call."

"Thank you," Nora said. "Somehow, I don't think I'll be hearing that from Corey."

"So how is the investment business going?"

"It's good. It's a little different when you're risking your own money, but it's still good."

Nora had taken part of her inheritance and given it to Lucy to invest. After hearing all the good things she had done for Tatty and Ed, she decided taking a risk with Lucy really wasn't a risk. "And how much have my savings doubled?"

"I'm working on it. Remember, long-term investments work best." It was such a novelty to have cash to invest that it was thrilling when Lucy came to tell her that she had increased her dividends.

"Has Corey said anything to you about our earnings from Brockwell Industries?"

"No. We were supposed to get a report last month. Every quarter, right?"

"That's what the lawyer said."

"Why do I feel like we're after him for child support?"

Nora added, "Why do I feel like he might be pocketing our earnings? It gets worse. He and Wiley are now working together to get our food shipments."

Lucy gasped. "Corey helping another human being? Corey is helping your hotel? Something's not right here."

"I know. Nothing is happening the way we expected. starting with Mr. Shaw's sudden death."

Evangeline had been quietly listening and finally joined in. "The Tunie has been around for so many years, it makes me wonder if this is the first murder."

Nora hadn't thought of that. Thousands of people had passed through the doors of the hotel. What secrets might be hidden there?

"If it does turn out to be a murder, it will be the first one... that we know of."

Lucy smiled. "You never know. If those walls could talk, right? I'm headed over to Shady Sunsets. Your grandmother has been asking about you."

"Tell her I'll see her at Tatty and Ed's anniversary dinner."

Nora hated putting her off and vowed she would make it up to her once the conference was over.

Chapter 27

The next morning, as Nora sipped her coffee behind the front desk of the hotel, Tuck walked through the lobby door. "I hear there was a big missing persons ... uh, cat case yesterday," he said. He clearly was acting like the embrace in the hallway had never happened. Nora wondered if she could do the same.

"How did you hear about it?"

"They were talking about it when I got into the office this morning."

"I'm surprised your old girlfriend didn't text you," Nora said. Tuck put on a lopsided grin and, looking to make sure there wasn't anyone else in the lobby, stepped behind the desk with Nora, taking her into his arms. "Now, I told you she was in my past. My distant past. She seems to have forgotten I was the one who broke it off with her, not the other way around." He gently placed the palm of his hand on Nora's cheek.

She looked up at him. He had such honest eyes. How could she doubt him? "You promise?"

"I promise by my oath as a lawman and an Eagle scout. Did you have to put up with her yesterday during the search?"

"Amazingly, no. I guess she doesn't do that kind of thing."

Tuck's police walkie-talkie sounded off on his belt. "Tuck. We need you back here at the station. Right away."

"Can it wait?"

There was a pause on the other end, and then the radio crackled. "No sir. We have a suspicious death."

"On my way." He tipped up Nora's chin and kissed her.

"Sorry about this. We were just getting to the good part."

"Go," Nora whispered, thankful that they were getting a little of what they had back. As she watched him exit, she wondered if Catpurnicus had ever been found. She came in at seven, and none of the guests had been up yet. She hoped that they would start coming down for breakfast soon.

Dominic came in holding a small camera. "It doesn't look like I got anything again. I think all this commotion is making the ghosts hide."

"I am more than willing to put up with a ghost for a few days of quiet," Nora said.

When Dominic volunteered to take over at the front desk, Nora decided to grab a few minutes to herself. She climbed the stairs to the fourth floor. Hidden away on this floor was an alcove that looked out on the main street of Piney Woods. When Nora first came to work at the hotel, the alcove was a long-neglected empty space, but she had suggested moving a comfy chair into one of the corners. Marty surprised her when she had one of the original chairs from the Tunie reupholstered in a soft velvety brown. Now it was one of Nora's favorite places to go and think. As she sank into her favorite chair, she tried to sort out her thoughts. Tuck was always present in the back of her mind, but she also wanted to get to the bottom of Alan Shaw's murder. While speaking with Camille Martin-Ortega yesterday, she was amazed that no one had said that Mr. Shaw had been murdered. She let her gaze drift out the window to Main Street. It was just another day in Piney Woods, with people visiting Dudley's Brew for a fresh cup of coffee and then strolling over to the library to pick up the latest best seller. The sun was shining, the birds were singing, and the church bells had just begun a rendition of Amazing Grace.

She tried to replay Alan Shaw's entrance at the Tunie. When she first saw him, he was ringing that bell. She asked him to join her at the front desk. He followed, and then, finding he did not have a reservation, she called Hickelby's Motor Lodge.

Nora's phone began to ring. Tuck's name was displayed on the caller ID. "Hey, where are you?"

"I'm at the hotel. Where are you?"

"I'm at the hotel. I just got here; only I don't see you anywhere." He sounded worried and impatient.

"I'm on the fourth floor. I'm in the alcove at the end of the hall."

"Okay. I can find that. Stay right where you are. I'll come up." A minute later, Tuck came out of the stairway door, panting slightly. Nora noted that he also didn't want to get back in that elevator.

Tuck's eyebrows furled as he came closer to her hiding place. His walk was efficient as he came near her. "What are you doing way up here?"

"I just needed some time to clear my head. Did they find Catpurnicus?" Nora said.

"Not that I know of. How well did you know Rick Stephenson?"

"Just that he's an investigative reporter who is trying to find out more about Alan Shaw's murder. Why are you speaking in the past tense?"

"One of the searchers stumbled over his body in a clump of trees on the edge of town. It looks like blunt force. A lot of blunt force in multiple areas."

"He was beat to death."

"More like crushed. If I had to guess, I would say he was hit or even run over by a car."

"The only reason he came here was because I called him. He worked for the magazine that Alan Shaw did the most freelance work for. I never expected him to fly here. Who rushes to the scene of a murder?" Nora hated to admit she was relieved that his death was in no way connected to the Tunie.

"When was the last time you saw Mr. Stephenson?"

"Yesterday. Here. He was going to go out and try to interview people from the convention to find out what Alan Shaw was investigating."

"I think we'd all like to know that. Looking at all theories, he might have just been run over by a drunk driver last night."

"That's true." Nora knew neither of them believed that theory for a minute, but she agreed anyway.

"Is there anything else you can tell me?"

"I was up here trying to go through Alan Shaw's attempt to check in to the hotel. He was angry because I was not at my post."

"Where were you?"

"I had just come back from straightening chairs in the dining room. Anyway, he was standing there by the..." Nora stopped as something occurred to her.

"I need to go." She rose from the chair.

Tuck's walkie-talkie squawked on his shoulder, and a tinny voice emitted from it, filling the empty hallway. "Tuck? We need you back at the crime scene."

"On my way," he said into the small black box. He turned to Nora. "Where are you going?"

"It could be nothing. I'll let you know." Nora took the stairs two at a time.

Chapter 28

As Nora came out of the stairway door on the first floor, Izzy Franklin was standing at the elevator waiting for a car. "Nora? I was on my way up to speak with you. The guy at the desk said you were on the fourth floor. I just wanted to take a moment to talk to you."

Nora's shoulders heaved from the exertion of coming down the stairs. "Yes?" She worried Izzy was here to file a complaint about her losing the manuscript. She couldn't blame her if she wanted to take such an action. "Listen, if it's about the manuscript, I thought we discussed that."

"It is. But it's not what you think. I'm here to apologize. You were stuck in an elevator, and I was wrong to go after you. Evangeline helped me to see that. Also, spending some time in the Piney Woods jail has made me reevaluate my anger issues. I hope that you will accept my apology."

This apology was a major change for Izzy. Had the little librarian been scared straight in the dinky Piney Woods jail? It was closer to the jail from *The Andy Griffith Show* than Riker's Island.

"That's very kind of you," Nora said in relief. She had liked Izzy before the manuscript incident. Her apology was welcome. Nora secretly cheered her on for going after Sasha LeClaire after Sasha's treatment of Evangeline. Now she wished that she had thrown a punch or two.

"I felt like I needed to do this because someone has shown me great kindness, and I can see what effect it has on another human being."

Nora smiled as her heart warmed. "Do you mean Evangeline?"

"Yes." Izzy brought her hands together in front. "She's read through some of my manuscript, and while it's not perfect and needs some work, she sees potential in it. Potential in me," she squeaked. "I am just so grateful that she spent that time with me."

"That's wonderful. I have to say I really admire the way you kept trying."

"One thing you learn when you're a writer is that you have to overcome obstacles and live with the ups and downs. No matter how many things seem overwhelming, you have to keep plowing on."

Nora liked Izzy's new attitude. It was something she needed to use in her own predicament. "Wow. How do you continue to feel motivated when you don't have somebody there supporting you?"

"Sometimes when things are bad, you have to keep thinking, working, and figuring out a way to make it work for you. That works for me better than ten people telling me what a good job I'm doing."

Nora mulled over what Izzy was saying. She had been putting out fires for so long that she had forgotten to look at everything that was in front of her. Izzy continued speaking, unaware of Nora's soul-searching.

"It really just takes focus. A lot of focus."

Nora knew what she was saying was right. She needed to quit bouncing off the external bumpers in this proverbial pinball game and just concentrate on getting through the convention.

Izzy gave her an expectant look, as if she were waiting for Nora to turn in an overdue book. "What were you doing? Is there a business office on the fourth floor?"

"I have a hunch about something. Something I overlooked that has to do with Alan Shaw's... accident."

"Don't you mean murder?"

Nora put a finger to her lip. "Shhh."

"Very good. You should consider working at the library. Listen, everybody in town thinks the guy was murdered. I don't think you're going to be able to sit on this much longer."

"Just as long as it doesn't come out until after the convention."

Comprehension came into Izzy's eyes. "Got it. Keepin' it on the down-low."

"Okay, I'll tell you, but you can't tell anybody else. Alan Shaw was not here to report on cats. He was here to interview somebody."

"Evangeline. Everyone knew that." So much for slowly revealing the truth, Nora thought.

"Okay, so you know about that. Somehow, I get the feeling that he was trying to smear Evangeline Cartwright. I think he had something on her, and I can't figure out what it was. He also wrote a bunch of mean reviews and an article slamming the hotel. He was a mean little man."

Izzy tapped her foot, ignited by Shaw's list of offenses. "What are we looking for?"

"Follow me."

When Nora and Izzy walked past the front desk, Dominic was busy directing a couple of guests to a drugstore. Nora zeroed in on the computer where Alan Shaw had been standing the first time she met him. Sure enough, there was a thumb drive sticking out of the USB slot on the side. With all that had been going on, no one had noticed it. None of the Meow Meetup guests had shown any interest in the computers, having brought their own laptops and tablets. Nora pulled up the contents of the drive on screen. There was one file on the thumb drive labeled "Sunshine Brigade." Nora opened up the file to find a collection of pictures and a Word document." She started going through the pictures and brought them up to full screen. The file was a collection of pictures of young people wearing fringed vests and holding signs protesting war. There were Volkswagen vans with peace signs and flowers painted on the side. The young people had long, stringy hair, and most of the men wore unkempt beards. One young woman in the picture was dancing around in a leather-fringed vest with a string of flowers in her hair. Why would Alan Shaw be interested in such an old story? The Vietnam War protests hadn't been news for fifty years. Maybe it was a story he was working on after he finished investigating Evangeline?

Izzy gasped, pointed to the screen, and then whispered.

"There she is."

"Who?"

Izzy turned back to the desk to make sure the hotel guests were not watching them. "Evangeline. She was part of the Sunshine Brigade."

"How are you getting that? She's about the right age to be a flower child, but a lot of people looked like that in the 1960s. Tatty and Ed met at Woodstock, for goodness' sake."

"What do you know about the Sunshine Brigade?" Izzy asked as she stepped back and folded her arms.

"Not a lot," Nora admitted. This wasn't just history to her, but ancient history. It was even before her mother's time.

Izzy nodded and began in her most scholarly reference desk voice, "They were an antiwar protest group. Not all the members were caught. They were responsible for an explosion that killed a janitor sleeping in the basement of a government building. I guess they thought the building was empty."

Nora looked back at the screen again. "He was trying to tell the world he found a member of the Sunshine Brigade, and you think it was our visiting mystery writer?" Nora had a tough time grasping this truth. Evangeline Cartwright was one of the nicest people she had ever met. If she had been a part of a violent protest group in the 1960s, it would have been a surprise.

"I guess he was. We can't tell anyone. It would ruin Evangeline." Once again, Izzy was willing to stand up for Evangeline, no matter what the cost.

Nora debated what she should do next. With all her vows about becoming a more trustworthy person, she knew she had to tell Tuck. She wanted some time to figure all of this out.

"At least not right now." Nora said. With this latest information, her head was spinning. There had been two murders since the Meow Meetup started, and both the victims just happened to be investigative reporters. If this was what they were on to, she also had to deduce that the person with the biggest motive was Izzy's hero. Evangeline Cartwright. The same hero that Tuck was about to question. She had to tell him before he met with her. He could be facing down a murderer.

Chapter 29

Izzy grabbed the thumb drive out of Nora's hand and slipped it into the pocket of her tweed skirt. "In my job, I've learned something valuable. Information is power. Until you are absolutely sure Evangeline is involved, this thumb drive will be locked up in the library. I will not have my inspiration railroaded by the local gendarme," Izzy told her.

"Izzy. Give me that. It doesn't belong to you." Nora extended her hand palm up.

"And last time I checked, it doesn't belong to you either."

How far would the little librarian go to protect her idol, Nora thought? Was she loyal enough to commit a murder? Was she now in league with the killer? Nora continued. "Be reasonable. This is evidence. I need to share this with the police."

A guest passed them, and Izzy waited for her to be well clear of their conversation. There was an edge in her voice when she whispered, "You can't do that. They'll arrest her for what was an impetuous time in her youth. For God sakes, it was the free-love sixties. Everyone gets a pardon for that time. Even without the valuable rehabilitation the prison would have given her, she turned out fine. Better than fine, she became the world's greatest mystery writer. Let the past be the past. Don't bring her down, sister. I promise I'll give it up, but for now, I'm keeping it," Izzy informed her.

Nora empathized with Izzy's deep connection to Evangeline and, like her, dismissed any notion of Evangeline posing a threat to society.

She also didn't see herself as Izzy's sister. Izzy made a quick exit just as Max and Marty joined Dominic at the front desk, stopping the conversation.

Sasha LeClaire came out of the elevator and placed her bill on the front desk, beginning her check-out process as she opened her soft black leather clutch. She had replaced her usual black attire with a tailored white suit, a white and black hat, and black patent leather heels with white accents.

"I hope you enjoyed your stay," Nora said through gritted teeth.

Sasha looked up, and a Cheshire cat grin came across her face. "Oh, my yes. I enjoyed my stay. There is nothing like reconnecting with old friends, with benefits." Her eyes shone with a deep feline glow as they challenged Nora.

"That's not what he said," Nora countered. She was not going to be put in her place by this alley cat. Being different from Izzy Franklin, she didn't need to hit her to strike a blow.

"Oh, I'm sure he told you some fanciful tale. Frankly, dear, you should look in the mirror. He is so out of your league," she purred.

Marty and Max exchanged glances, not saying a word. They waited for the next exchange between the two women.

Nora shook her head. "I don't believe you."

"Believe what you want, my dear. I will have fond memories of Piney Woods, and it will have nothing to do with the smell of cows or dried-up oil wells." Sasha pulled a pair of black sunglasses out of her bag, put them on, and turned for the door. "Ciao, baby."

Max covered his hand with his mouth, holding in a laugh. "Wow, Nora. What happened?"

Dominic, who had been there the day Nora found Tuck and Sasha in an embrace, gave a knowing smile. "I know all about it. Of course, I am a trained observer."

"It was nothing. She and Tuck knew each other in college. Tuck told me she came onto him, not the other way around."

Marty came around and put a protective arm around Nora. "And now I know why you were asking about his dating life. That's my Tuck. He is always a gentleman."

"Maybe she drugged him and used his body without a thought," Max said, his eyes getting a little dreamy.

"I don't want to talk about it. How is everything going?"

"No problems if you don't count the second dead guy they just found." Dominic reached under the counter to retrieve a hard-backed book on demonology. "Now that my relief is here, I think I'll go see what's cooking in the kitchen. If they only knew how to make my mother's veal parmesan." He took off toward the kitchen, whistling.

Marty leaned forward and lowered her voice. "Even with this latest death, many of the guests are talking about coming back and visiting Piney Woods on vacation. I guess we are now an official vacation destination."

"And don't forget the smell of cows and dried-up oil wells."

"Then Sasha did get to some of the local attractions," Max said under his breath.

"Stop, Max," Marty said, hitting him on the arm. Max reddened at her attention. She turned to Nora. "Do they know anything about this second death?"

"Tuck thinks someone might have run him over with a car."

"Ouch!" Max winced.

"He was looking for someone to interview. He really wanted to talk to Evangeline, but I don't think he talked to her."

"You know, Mrs. Martin-Ortega told me that she was going to book a cat breeder to be the keynote speaker, but then Evangeline Cartwright called her and volunteered," Marty said. "She came all the way from New York City to our little town in Texas. It couldn't have worked out any better for us."

"Maybe we should comp her room?" Max suggested.

"We aren't that grateful," Marty said as she took a piece of paper off the printer. "Right now, at the Tunie, every paid bill helps. Besides that, I'm sure it will be paid for by the Meow Meetup convention funds. No freebies and no discounts. Evangeline requested her bill."

Nora liked the sound of that. She would have to get Tatty to embroider it for the lobby. She nodded. "You're right. Absolutely. Would you like for me to slip that under her door?" Nora wanted to have an excuse to talk to Evangeline anyway, especially after taking so much time away from the convention with her investigation of Mr. Shaw.

"Would you?" With everything that had happened to the elevator, Nora hadn't seen neither Max nor Marty get into the thing. The guests, however, blindly boarded the potential death trap. She started toward the elevator, thinking about Izzy. Although she and the librarian had come to a truce, she couldn't rule Izzy out as a suspect. She was fiercely protective of her mentor writer, but was it enough to take out a balding, obnoxious reporter? If Nora could just keep her focus, then maybe she could figure out what was going on and what really happened to Alan Shaw. Considering the information he was collecting on that thumb drive, she now felt sure he was murdered.

"Excuse me." Nora bumped into Mrs. Martin-Ortega, who had planted herself right in her path. She looked vastly different from what she had upon checking in. There were now faint purple bags under her eyes, and she seemed to have a cold.

Nora startled. "I'm sorry. I didn't see you there."

"Maybe you should look up when you walk. I was checking our billing for the convention. There seem to be some substantial errors on your part, not at all surprising with your one-star status." She flipped the paper directly into Nora's face. "I'll need you to fix it to reflect the accurate discount promised to us."

Nora felt the anger bubbling up in her. This woman had been demanding and condescending. "The bill is accurate." Her statement was short and to the point, but lost on Camille Martin-Ortega.

"You know what I'm talking about. We came here thinking that you were a five-star hotel. We experienced inaccurate menus, a death because of faulty equipment, and a local causing a disruption in the dining room over our keynote speaker. I know Texas is considered the Wild West, but we were promised the mild West. This is a one-star establishment, and we are compensating you based on what your hotel is worth."

"The one-star ratings were a malicious attack on the Tunie by a man who described places he had never been. And if that man were alive, we would be suing him for slander."

"I guess pushing him down the elevator shaft was so much more efficient for you. At the risk of my own personal safety, we will either pay the discounted price or not pay at all. Do you understand me, or do I need to speak more slowly?" Once again, she took a condescending tone toward Nora.

"I discussed it with my partner." Nora looked over at Marty, who was still standing at the front desk with Max. She hadn't realized it, but they had been listening intently to the conversation. Nora gave Marty a look to come over and help, but Marty simply returned a thumbs-up. Camille Martin-Ortega was formidable, even to Marty. Nora was on her own.

She took a breath, determined not to be undermined by the convention organizer. "If you wish to break the contractual agreement that we have, we will be glad to take you to court for trying to skip out on your hotel bill. Oh, and good luck trying to book another hotel for next year. Hotel managers are famous for sharing information about their most troublesome groups with other hotel managers. It's sort of a free therapy thing, seeing as we don't get paid enough. Pay in full, or we'll see you in court."

Mrs. Martin-Ortega started to open her mouth but then found she had nothing to say. Nora stormed past the elevator and off to the stairway, slamming the door behind her. She felt so much rage that climbing four sets of stairs would be the best thing for her. Once she was on the other side of the door and out of the vision of Mrs. Martin-Ortega, she took a deep breath before starting her climb. Had she really told off the organizer of the Meow Meetup? She wasn't sure, but she thought she had. She might have just committed professional suicide, but something inside of her had burst. Once it started coming out, she found it was difficult to stop. Camille Martin-Ortega had been angling for a discount she didn't deserve. Nora clutched Evangeline's bill and started climbing the steps. When she got to the top floor, she had to place her hands on her knees to take a quick breath. She would not need membership in a gym if she kept using the stairs instead of the elevator. As her hands rested on her knees, she noticed that the cleaning staff was still not vacuuming under the end tables that rested next to the elevator. There was a small piece of white fluff lodged in the corner, and she bent over to grab it. She examined the white fluff. It resembled something that she had seen earlier this week. She stuffed it into her pocket and knocked on Evangeline's door.

Nora's cell phone rang in her pocket as she awaited Evangeline's answer. Marty was shouting through the phone, "Nora, get down here. The Meow Meetup organizer just passed out. She sprawled out on the floor in the conference room."

Chapter 30

Nora rushed down the stairwell. "What happened?" Camille Martin-Ortega was gasping for breath in the middle of the conference room.

Marty was next to her, cell phone in hand. "It looks like she is having a serious asthma attack. We've called an ambulance."

Nora got down on the floor and took Camille's hand. "Camille, do you have asthma? Do you have an inhaler somewhere?"

Camille's body heaved, struggling so much for breath that she couldn't answer. Nora looked around. "Her purse. Does anyone know where her purse is?"

One of the convention goers brought a brown leather bag over from a side table. Upon seeing it, Nora remembered Camille standing next to it speaking into her phone not too long ago. She rummaged through the bag but did not find anything that could help Camille. When she touched the screen of the phone, it lit up before her.

Bubby Tidwell led the ambulance crew as they thundered into the room. Instead of the normal reflective fire gear, Buddy had on the uniform of an emergency medical technician. "How are you, Miss Nora? Hopin' I get my next rescue on the books today." Buddy was famous for rescuing the townspeople of Piney Woods. He even rescued Nora once and would never let her forget it. He focused in on Camille, gasping on the floor. "Hi there, ma'am. I'm Bubby Tidwell, and you can calm down now. I've rescued half this town, including ol' Nora here."

He pulled a small box from his bag, attached a mask, and then fastened it to Camille's face. He then turned to the crowd that was watching him and spoke like a first-aid tour guide. "Don't worry. Your friend will be fine in just a few minutes. No need to panic. We have it all under control."

Nora watched the entire scene but couldn't stay. She had a hunch, and right now would be the perfect time to check it out. She pulled Camille's room key out of her bag. "I'm going to head upstairs to see if she has an inhaler up there."

"Okay, boss," Max saluted. Marty's smile reassured Nora that she was grateful for her leadership in a crisis. Nora headed up the stairs to the next floor. Panting for breath, she quickly opened the door to 213.

A guest from 211 poked her head out, bedecked in blue plastic curlers. "What is going on?"

"Mrs. Martin-Ortega had an asthma attack. I'm looking for an inhaler."

The guest from 211 gasped and went inside her room. A second later, she re-entered the hall, carrying a handbag over her arm and a scarf over her head. "I'll just go check on her." Like many people, she couldn't resist slowing down for an accident.

When Nora entered, she found the room empty except for one surprise. Catpurnicus, in all his glory, was nonchalantly licking his paw resting on the neatly made bed. What was he doing in Camille Martin-Ortega's room? The implications of his presence here would have to be resolved later. Even though he had been away from his owner for days now, he seemed extremely content. Was he on some sort of kitty Xanax for his nerves? Why was this cat still here?

"Here, Kitty Kitty."

Catpurnicus gave Nora a disinterested stare and then purred. He appeared to be a nice cat now that he was out of his cat carrier, as Nora had seen him earlier. Leaning over the bed and reaching for the cat, her hand grew closer to the gentle rumbling, but then the purring turned to a low-pitched growl. She reached out to grab the cat, but Catpurnicus swiped at her with a claw. Did the cat think she was playing?

"It's okay, boy. It's okay." She reached out once again, and this time Catpurnicas scrambled under the bed. This was one of the few rooms where they had not installed blocker boards under the bed to keep guests from losing electronics and stray items of clothing. The cat settled into the middle of the space underneath the box spring.

"Here, Kitty, Kitty." Catpurnicus ignored Nora. It was obvious he was going to be under the bed, and she was free to go on her way. If she couldn't get the cat to come willingly, maybe she could lure him out. Looking around the room, Nora found a cat toy that consisted of a ribboned stick with a pink feathery bird on the end and a bag of cat food. Grabbing both, she crawled to the underside of the bed to look at the cat. First, she held out the toy, wiggling it a bit.

"Hey, Catpurnicus, don't you want to play?" Her voice was artificially sweet as she tried to coax the reluctant feline. Catpurnicus was not in the least interested, no matter how goofy she sounded.

"Fine." Nora held out her hand with food in it, and Catpurnicus flinched. "Doesn't this look delicious? Come on, baby, I got a whole bag of this stuff." Nora waved it around a little more. The small brown kibble looked about as appetizing as a handful of erasers, but there was no doubt the finicky cat was interested. Catpurnicus started scooting toward the edge of the bed, and when he was close enough for Nora to grab, she reached out and pulled him into the daylight. Even though she was sure she hadn't hurt him, Catpurnicus growled at her as her arms closed around him. Nora started feeding him the cat food that he had given up his freedom for. Grabbing another handful of food from the stiff paper bag, she exited the room with her unhappy charge. As she went down the steps with the cat, her nose began to tickle. By the time she opened the door, the urge to sneeze had become overwhelming.

Max, who was standing on the edge of the dining room, turned around. "You found the cat! That's wonderful." Before Nora could give him any kind of greeting, an enormous sneeze exploded out of her. Catpurnicus took the sneeze as an opportunity to jump ship. He immediately ran in the direction of the kitchen.

Nora ran into the dining room, where Catpurnicas kept appearing and disappearing under the white tablecloths. "Oh no. It took me forever to catch him upstairs," Nora said, sniffing after her double sneeze.

"And I suppose you want me to catch him?"

As far as she was concerned, she had done enough for that stupid cat, but letting him run could cause a negative review. "Why don't we both go after him? Remember, we're trying to keep the one-star reviews to a minimum."

"Yes, because a death in the elevator shaft isn't enough for anyone to write a rotten review. Where did you find him?"

"Camille Martin-Ortega's room."

"Dang. This is getting interesting."

The cat seemed to be enjoying his own version of "Whack-a-Mole" as Max and Nora chased him.

"Man, he's fast," Max said, saying the obvious.

"You think?"

"I hate to bring this up, but there is also the little thing that the health inspector said. We shouldn't have animals in the kitchen or dining room area. If he were to come back by, we could be in even deeper trouble."

Marty and Wiley appeared as Bubby Tidwell wheeled Camille out of the banquet room on a stretcher. "Hey there, Bubby," Wiley said, acknowledging the star of the fire department.

"Hey, Wiley. Mark it down. Rescued another." Wiley looked down to find Catpurnicus rubbing up against his pant leg, now fresh from his hiding place.

"Hey there, little fella. Where did you come from?" Where Catpurnicus had treated Nora and Max with nothing but disdain, he seemed to have a soft spot for Wiley.

"Pick him up, Uncle Wiley. We've been trying to catch him."

Uncle Wiley did as instructed and picked up the cat gently. His eyes crinkled in the corners as he smiled. "I'd like to call myself the cat whisperer, but it's the way I smell. Wouldn't you come running after a man who smells like bacon and fried chicken?" He handed the cat to Nora.

Bubby's ears perked up. "Is that the cat the whole town has been looking for? Darn, I wanted to be the one to find him."

"Cats don't count," Tuck said. Nora wasn't sure when he had shown up.

"Tuck. Did you hear about Camille on the police radio?"

"Yes, I did. I'm just here to check on my favorite crisis-filled hotel. I see you found the cat. I'll cancel the BOLO."

Camille, who had been resting quietly under the oxygen mask, now reared up.

"Yes, we found him, Camille," Nora said. "What is more interesting is where we found him."

Camille became more agitated, and Bubby turned his attention to her. "All right now, little Missy. Just breathe deep, and ol' Bubby will have you right in no time."

Chapter 31

Tuck's eyebrows raised slightly. "Why do I think there's more to this than a cat out for a lark?"

"Yes. I'm going to lock him in the office until we find his owner. I think she's still out combing the streets with some of the other convention members. I'm pretty sure Camille kidnapped—I mean, catnapped him."

"Could it be that she found the cat and was keeping it until she got ahold of the owner?" Tuck said as he followed Nora and closed the door behind him.

Nora let the boxy red cat onto the floor. "I don't think so. I was talking to this Camille yesterday, and she didn't mention anything about finding the cat. I did find it interesting, though, that she never joined the searchers. She seemed to be on her phone most of the time."

"Why would she do that?"

"Doug told us that a cat like this has a stud fee in the thousands of dollars."

Tuck stroked his chin. "Lucky guy."

"There's more." Nora thought of the thumb drive in Izzy's pocket. "I may have information on someone who had a motive to kill Alan Shaw."

"I'm listening."

Nora stepped into the office and closed the door. "The only problem is that Izzy has it." Tuck drew nearer to Nora, making her feel a mixture of warmth and regret to have him so close. She could feel his breath on her neck.

"Has what?"

"A thumb drive. I was going to give it to you, but she pocketed it before I could. She's fierce about protecting Evangeline."

"Evangeline?"

"It's complicated, but I promise the next time I see her, I'll wrestle her to the floor to get it."

"She's stronger than she looks. You'd better be careful."

Nora laughed. "Oh, and by the way, your old girlfriend checked out."

"She did? So soon?"

Nora took a breath. "I thought you didn't care about her anymore."

"I don't. I'm still investigating a murder. Having all the potential suspects here, makes it more convenient for me to figure out who killed Mr. Shaw."

"And possibly Mr. Stephenson."

"I guess somebody doesn't believe in the free press around here."

Nora shook her head. "And now we have a catnapping."

"This place is going to hell in a handbasket," Tuck said.

"I'll admit, it seems like we have a lot going on right now."

Tuck's eyebrows were raised. "You have been soaking up all the city's police services."

"Okay, Officer Way-Too-Friendly, here are the facts. We've had a catnapping."

"Strange but true."

"We've had deliberate sabotage of our restaurant operations."

"And you feel that Jumbo Jim and Moore Foods have been in cahoots."

"Correct, but Wiley has found a solution to that problem."

"One less for me." Tuck's lips curled into a smile. "You certainly have done your police work. You have suspects all over the place. What about Big Dudley and Little Dudley? They're a treacherous pair. Getting the whole town addicted to caffeine over at Dudley's Brew? Is this a citywide restaurant conspiracy, or is it just Jumbo Jim, the mastermind? Maybe we should check the donut shop? Were they in on it too? You have to get up early to really get to know those guys."

Nora ignored Tuck's attempt at humor. "Jumbo Jim has been trying to stop our restaurant from operating ever since we landed the Meow Meetup convention. I'm pretty sure he's the one behind our delayed shipments from Moore Foods, and I suspect he sent a couple of Hades Alley bikers here on false pretenses to release cockroaches in the dining room. He's desperate. No matter what he does to us, we will keep going."

"More importantly, the Piney Woods PD has had to investigate not one, but two murders connected with the convention."

"Cat people." Nora sighed. "They seem so soft and fluffy that you never notice the claws."

Tuck softened. "Okay. Good enough, although why you had all this happening and didn't tell me, I'll never know."

"You were busy. You had a meeting in Lubbock, and then we were keeping you occupied with poor Mr. Shaw falling down the elevator. Then, of course, you were also whooping it up with that alley cat."

Tuck held up a hand to prevent her from continuing. "Enough. I already explained that what you think never happened."

"Funny, that's not what she said."

Tuck blushed. "Really?"

"She made it sound pretty passionate."

"I told you. She's in the past. I broke up with her, and I'm surprised she even remembered me."

"Any port in a storm," Nora said.

"I guess. So tell me, what have you been doing while I've been out of town? Have you taken up reading Evangeline Cartwright's mystery novels? Has being around the mystery author all weekend caused you to think in terms of plots and red herrings?"

"Which brings me to who might have killed Alan Shaw."

Nora paused for a moment as Izzy's face flashed before her. She wanted to help her protect Evangeline, but she was also not keen on a murderer going about his or her business in her hotel. It was tough, but the right thing to do was to tell him. "You need to check out Evangeline Cartwright."

"Why would I need to check her out? I think your imagination is starting to run away with you. This is a nice little old lady who writes mysteries about pie-judging contests. She is not exactly the typical FBI profile of a murderer."

"Trust me; consider it. I'm telling you this even though I promised Izzy I wouldn't. I can't get around this creepy feeling that it might be her."

"All right." Tuck grumbled and stroked his chin as he considered the option. Catpurnicus, who had been under the desk, growled at Tuck. Maybe the cat was on Nora's side, or maybe they were just too grumpy males unhappy with the world.

Tatty opened the door to the office. "Nora? Did you find the cat?"

"Oh, yes. Sorry, I should have called." Nora apologized.

"Ed should be along shortly. He was picking up his suit for the anniversary party." Tatty's eyes drifted from Nora to Tuck, unsure of what she had just walked in on. Tuck turned toward Tatty but made himself busy by pulling out his policeman's notebook. He began to write a note and then snapped it closed.

"Close the door. Don't let the cat out. Thank you so much for helping out in our search. It turns out he was in one of the hotel rooms all along."

"Are you kidding? I have to go tell the altar guild at St. Mary's. We had them searching in the blocks around the church."

Nora walked over and took Tatty's arm. "Thank you again."

As they entered the lobby, Doug was escorting Evangeline out of the elevator. Tuck, who had been following Nora and Tatty, now stepped forward and greeted Evangeline as she exited the sliding doors. Nora was surprised Doug had breached etiquette and made it to the fourth floor, even if it was to escort her somewhere.

"Miss Cartwright, I was wondering if I could ask you a couple of questions?" Tuck asked politely. Evangeline's eyes widened. Doug leaned toward Evangeline, and his shoulder touched hers as he folded his arms in front of his chest.

"You want to ask me questions?" Evangeline asked with a look of surprise on her face.

"Yes ma'am. If you wouldn't mind," Tuck said.

Tatty cocked her head to the side as she looked at Evangeline. Her eyes reshaped into slits as she observed the mystery writer. "Excuse me, but have we met somewhere before?"

Evangeline's eyes scanned Tatty's face. "I don't believe so."

Tatty continued to stare. "I never forget a face. That is up until now."

Evangeline's response was always gracious. "And you are so lucky to be able to do that. I'm so sorry, I'm not making the connection." She turned to Tuck. "What did you want to know?"

"I'd better get going," Tatty said, but as she walked away, she turned back for one last look at Evangeline and then shook her head. She stopped and snapped her fingers as she remembered something. "I still need to go by Shady Sunsets and pick up the place cards Rosalyn was making for us. Your grandmother does the most beautiful calligraphy. I'm just glad she can still do it. I'm sure people will keep their cards after the party. They turn out so pretty."

Wiley was just coming into the lobby, dishrag in hand. "She would love to hear that. She does beautiful work."

Nora thought about the quiet that surrounded Shady Sunsets. The thought of visiting her grandmother appealed to her. Maybe she could get some peace about all that was going on with the hotel, with Tuck, and even with Jumbo Jim.

"I can pick them up for you if you like."

Tatty looked surprised but then uttered, "Oh, would you, dear? I really hate to ask after all you've had to do here. It would be a real help to me."

"I'd enjoy seeing my grandmother."

Tatty patted Nora's arm. "And she would enjoy seeing you."

After Tatty left, Wiley started to make a quick exit for the door.

"Don't even think about it," Nora said after her uncle as she followed him into the kitchen. She had faced down Camille Martin-Ortega, and now she felt a sense of empowerment. She was finding dealing with things less painful than not dealing with them.

Wiley looked at her innocently. "Uh, did you need something? I was going to get some supplies for the clean-up."

"You can get those in a minute, Uncle Wiley. I've thought a lot about this, and I'd just like to know what would ever possess you to ask Corey for help."

Wiley pulled at his ear and gave Nora a quick smile. "It's personal."

This was not the answer she expected. Ever since Wiley McArdle came into her life, their relationship had been a little strange. The first time she laid eyes on him, he fell into a trash can in a drunken stupor. Once a person has shown that side of themselves, it is difficult to see that person any other way. Most people want to show their put-together selves first. Wiley did just the opposite. "When you say it's personal, you make me think you have some sort of friendship with my stepbrother. You don't even like the guy, so spare me on the personal stuff."

"Trust me on this, Nora. I really can't talk about it."

One more time, someone was asking for her blind trust. First Tuck, and now Wiley. How much going along was she willing to do with these men she loved? "Okay, I'll make a compromise. You don't have to tell me all about your new BFF, Corey, but you do need to fill me in on the business side of it. Why Brockwell Industries? How much is it costing us? How often will they deliver?"

Wiley nodded his head as he listened to each question roll by. Exuberance came into his voice. "Fair enough. Yes, these shipments are coming through the warehousing operations of Brockwell Industries. They are actually costing us less than that highway robbery outfit of Moore Foods, and they will deliver as often as I order."

This sounded like a dream come true, but Nora's questions were leading to more. Why hadn't she ever thought of using the warehouse operations her father had set up? "How did you negotiate a deal like this, Uncle Wiley? This is so much better than the arrangement we had with Moore Foods."

"Like I said, it's personal, but I'm glad you approve."

Nora felt exasperation rising with this man. He wanted her to trust him. He wanted her to treat him as an uncle, which he was, but he only wanted her to know what he wanted her to know. She was tired of being held at arm's length. "Wiley, you need to tell me what's going on. What if Corey comes back and tries to cheat us out of the hotel? That's how he works, you know."

"He won't."

"How do you know? When did Corey Brockwell ever do anything nice for anyone? He's an entitled, rich kid with a gambling problem. For everyone's sake, you need to come clean."

"Stop," Wiley said, raising a broken voice to Nora. She was startled by his sudden temper, but knew she had been egging him on. Caesar, who had been chopping vegetables, looked up from his work.

"I'll tell you, but you're not going to like it."

Nora feared she would now find out the details of Wiley's dance with the devil. She worried they might never be able to set it right.

"I am working with Corey in more than one way."

"What?" Nora snapped.

"We are part of the same addiction group."

"Isn't he a gambling addict?" Nora asked.

"We're a small town. We have to lump the addictions together. Sort of a one-stop shopping kind of thing. Corey is my sponsor."

"What kind of sponsor?"

"You know. When I feel like I need a drink, I call him."

"And he lays bets on whether you'll succumb?" Nora quipped. She instantly knew she'd gone too far.

Wiley turned from her and walked away. "Wiley, I'm sorry."

He pushed his bony hand through the air to wave her off. He was done talking.

Chapter 32

When Nora re-entered the lobby, Camille Martin-Ortega stood in front of the check-in desk with her hands on her well-toned hips. The dark circles had vanished from under her eyes.

"Glad to see they fixed you up so quickly," Nora said.

"It's amazing they had competent medical staff out here in the sticks," she acknowledged. Piney Woods did have good doctors, not to mention Bubby with his rescue tally. Camille raised her chin. "You had no right to barge into my hotel room. I should call the police for breaking and entering."

Nora smiled as she watched the ever-controlled convention manager start to squirm. One of her tiny pin curls bobbed off her forehead when she spoke in tones that were becoming more and more shrill. A couple of convention guests walked by. Now that the cat search had been called off, there were a few classes being held in the conference room, including litter box control and fur ball relief. "Funny, you should mention calling the police. They already know. I would expect a phone call. They have a few questions to ask you after they spent days of manpower looking for a cat that was never lost. What were you doing with Catpurnicus in your room?"

Camille's breath caught, and then she resumed her stance. "I don't know what you're talking about."

One of the guests turned and smiled. "That's wonderful news! You found Catpurnicus?"

"No," Camille growled.

"Yes," Nora said cheerily.

"Where was he?"

"In Mrs. Martin-Ortega's room. I suspect he was there the whole time."

Now the guest looked confused. "Why would he be in your room while we were all out searching?"

"Not all of you were searching. Mrs. Martin-Ortega chose to stay here, making phone calls. If I had to guess, she was calling to set up a few dozen stud appointments before Catpurnicus would magically reappear."

"Don't be ridiculous." Camille sniped.

"Did someone say Catpurnicus?" Mitzy Olson, the cat's pink-haired owner, now stood at the door. One of the guests had retrieved her from one of the informational classes on litter box care and now stood with her arm linked in hers.

"Good news. He's safe. I found him upstairs in Mrs. Martin-Ortega's room."

The look on Mitzy's face registered from confusion to anger. "You took him? You took my Purny?"

She ran to Camille and claws out, attacked her. Camille screamed as she hit the floor, and Tuck quickly returned from the dining room with Evangeline. This time, he didn't have to pull the women apart as Camille cowered against the wall.

"Get her away from me. Yes, I took her stupid cat. Why should someone with pink hair get all that money just for having a promiscuous cat? Tell me that. It's just not fair."

The ruckus caused Marty to limp over and try to pull Mitzy off Camille.

"Just what is the sentence for catnapping?" Marty said this over Mitzi's yelling.

"Life. Nine times." Nora answered.

Chapter 33

The hallways of Shady Sunsets Nursing Home and Assisted Living Facility had the familiar smell of cafeteria food and the wisps of old-fashioned cologne, like Evening in Paris. After all that had happened, Nora was glad to get the chance to get away. When she looked in on her grandmother, Rosalyn, she was sitting with another resident in the parlor watching Jeopardy.

"Beatrix Potter," the other woman, a stout lady wearing a blue bathrobe, shouted at the TV.

"Beatrix Potter," repeated Rosalyn just a split second later.

Arnette Cooper, Lucy's mother, stood in the background, her arms crossed. She wore a bright pink flowered scrub top with black pants. She was laughing at Rosalyn and her Jeopardy buddy and smiled upon seeing Nora. "Every day, it never fails. They play along. If Alex Trebek had any brains at all, he would tour the nursing homes. It would be quite a showdown." Arnette chuckled.

When Alex Trebek confirmed their answer, the bathrobe lady clapped her hands together, making a hollow sound. Rosalyn beamed with a satisfied smile on her face. "I knew it. I knew it all along."

"Knew what?" Nora asked.

"Beatrix Potter wrote *The Tale of Mr. Jeremy Fisher*. I used to read it to your mother." Her features softened. She had once had the vibrant red hair that Nora sported today. Rosalyn's hair had now turned a beautiful, silky white, framing her soft face. "And hello to you, pretty girl." Rosalyn reached out her thin arms, and Nora came into them for a hug. "What brings you out here today?"

"Tatty sent me for the place cards."

"Oh yes, I have them in my room." She reached for her walker but then turned back to the bathrobe lady. "You'll just have to win the rest of the questions without me."

"Just like every other day," the woman joked.

As they made their way down the hall, Rosalyn concentrated on the steady motion of each step. "I heard about all that hulabaloo you have going on over at the hotel. Did a man really fall down the elevator shaft?"

"Yes, he did."

"And I heard you were stuck in the elevator, too? I can't tell you how many times I've been in that elevator. I never thought of it as a killer," Rosalyn said.

"I know. I should have called. Sorry, you had to hear about it secondhand. Have you spoken with Uncle Wiley lately?" Nora still felt guilty over assuming Wiley had fallen off the wagon. She admitted to herself that she hadn't been supportive enough of his recovery process, but the idea of working with Corey seemed crazy to her. He had to be the world's worst possible choice for a sponsor. He didn't have any self-control over his own actions.

"Some. He's been so busy with his work, you know. I'm bursting my buttons that my granddaughter and my son are working together so well. It's like we have a family business. I tell everyone here who will listen to me. Your mama would have been over the moon about it. Wiley has been living on the fringe of this town for years, and people have laughed at him. That breaks a mother's heart. You changed all that. I'm thankful for the day you showed up here full of spunk, and I immediately recognized that red hair of your mother's. I took one look at you and knew my daughter was coming back to me."

When Nora arrived in Piney Woods, she was surrounded by family, yet she never knew it. The first time she ran into Rosalyn, they passed in the hall, and her striking resemblance to Kay Alexander, Rosalyn's daughter, caused the older woman to have to sit down.

"Tatty is so busy getting ready for the anniversary party that I offered to come over for the guest cards for the place settings."

"You have enough going on right now. You shouldn't have volunteered."

"To tell you the truth, I wanted to step away from the hotel for a bit."

Rosalyn nodded and pulled a white business envelope out of her desk drawer. It was packed with tiny white cards with the names of Tatty's guests intricately lettered on them in fine black ink. "That was quite a list Tatty gave me. Everybody and their plumber are going to be at this shindig. I hope you and Wiley can have the Tunie ready after the cat people."

"We're trying. It's been wild, but we can still do the anniversary party."

"Child, what is the matter with you? Is something going on with Wiley? Has he said something to hurt your feelings?"

"I'm fine. We had an argument, and I said some things I probably shouldn't have. He's trying to stay sober, but in the process, he did something I don't approve of. I just feel like he's made a mistake."

"You're talking in riddles, sweetheart. What kind of mistake?"

"He made Corey Brockwell our food supplier. We were being cheated by the company we were using, and this was his solution. The Brockwell's have never done anything to help this family."

Rosalyn took a breath and settled her soft hands in her lap, laying them one on top of the other. "Sometimes, to solve a problem, a person has to think outside the realms of what they deem to be acceptable. Being in league with Adam's son, Corey, is certainly something we would all think of as a poor idea. Still, though, Wiley felt it was the only way out. Give it time, Nora. Maybe he was right. If he's wrong, then you were right, and you can tell him that over and over. That's what family is for."

"I suppose. We are getting our food shipments and not being messed with by our supplier. There's more, though, and I'm afraid I didn't handle this well either. Not only is Corey our new food wholesaler, but he's Uncle Wiley's addiction sponsor."

"He is? Mr. Brockwell's boy?"

"I know. I was shocked when Wiley told me. There is very little about Corey Brockwell that I find redeeming."

"I can see that."

Nora looked at one of the cards Rosalyn had prepared. Her grandmother's handiwork was exquisite, but the words began to blur as Nora's eyes filled with tears. "I just don't know what I'm going to do," she whispered.

Rosalyn reached over and stroked Nora's hair. "You'll keep on moving through this. That's all you can do. When you get a chance, try to find something you like that Wiley is doing. He's heard plenty of what you don't like. It will be hard, but after a while, if I know my boy, you two will find a way."

As Nora left Shady Sunsets, she felt a grayness passing through her soul. This whole week, starting with Alan Shaw's death and ending with her argument with Wiley, had left her depressed. Her mind drifted to Tuck. Trust issues. Sexy cat ladies. Rick Stephenson's death. Maybe her grandmother was right, and she needed to take her uncle's answer and work in a way that she had formerly deemed unacceptable. They sure didn't have anybody else lined up to deliver chicken.

Nora knew now what she needed to do, and it would start with a phone call to Tuck.

Chapter 34

When Nora arrived at the final gathering of the Meow Meetup, she had run by the bed and breakfast to change into a deep blue velvet cocktail dress. She pulled her hair up into a French roll, changing her look from efficient to stunningly beautiful.

"Wow, Nora. You look fabulous," Max said as he handed a glass of sparkling wine from the buffet table.

As much as Nora would have liked to guzzle down a couple of those glasses of wine, she decided she needed a clear head. "I'll pass. I'm working."

"I admire your professionalism. I, too, am working. All the more reason." Max downed the drink he had offered her.

"Has it been that bad?"

"No, not really, especially if you don't count the dead guy in the elevator shaft, I would say it was a seamless convention."

Wiley and his crew had done a beautiful job setting up a buffet on crisp white table linens with sandwiches along with tiny quiches, cheese, and crackers, twice-baked potatoes, and stuffed avocados stacked in pyramids on each side of the display. Wiley's talent had been wasted for so many years, and she was thankful to have him working for her now.

Izzy entered from the lobby wearing a black evening dress that hung loosely around the neck, making it look a size too big for her. Her collar bone protruded slightly as it held up a string of oversized pearls. She had also pulled her hair up, but instead of a French roll, she had haphazardly clipped on a rhinestone butterfly barrette. She wasn't a card-carrying member of this convention, but no one seemed to notice. Nora had to assume she wanted to get one last meeting with her mentor, Evangeline. Izzy was fiercely protective of Evangeline, and she couldn't be sure if Izzy was crazy enough to kill for her. Even if she was, she couldn't have known Alan Shaw's real reason for being at the convention. If she did kill Alan Shaw, it was a crime of passion. Somebody who worked in the library could be very passionate about the volumes of the author that they loved. Izzy picked up a glass of wine, looked around, and poured it down her throat in an awkward gesture.

No one was talking to the little librarian, so Nora walked over to welcome her. "Izzy! I didn't know you were coming to the party."

"I, uh, wasn't really invited. I hope that's all right." There was something different about Izzy, and it took Nora a moment to realize she wasn't wearing her glasses. Izzy was squinting, her gaze just slightly off center.

"That's fine," Max said as he joined them. "You can come as my guest."

Izzy looked at Max's giant frame and stated it flatly. "I'm not your date."

Max took her insult in stride. "I never said you were a date. I called you my guest. I was just being hospitable. That's kind of what we do here, if you hadn't noticed."

Izzy thought for a moment and then said, "Thanks."

One of the guests spilled a plate nearby and Max went over to help them pick up the stray food. After he left, Nora whispered in Izzy's ear. "I was wondering if you still had that little item."

Izzy nodded. "Right here." She produced the thumb drive from a side pocket in her ill-fitting gown.

"Good," Nora said. "I need to borrow it."

"Are you kidding?"

"I need you to trust me on this. I promise to give it back as soon as I'm finished with it."

Izzy eyed her. "Why should I trust you?"

"Why wouldn't you trust me? If I planned to do something to hurt Evangeline, I would have never let you take it. One night. That's all I need."

Izzy searched Nora's eyes. "One night. That's all?"

"Yes."

Izzy handed the thumb drive over.

"Thank you. You're not going to like this, but I told Tuck about it. Don't worry. He doesn't know all the details."

Izzy didn't look happy with that news but nodded in agreement. "I don't know what you're up to, but I'm trusting you."

Max returned as Izzy finished speaking. He looked confused, but smiled and took another sip of wine.

"Where did you get that dress?" Nora hoped her question didn't sound impolite.

She put her hands on the neckline of the dress and yanked it up. "Goodwill. There is not much call for the party circuit in the reference section of the library. I paid six dollars for it. I hope I can return it after this."

"They will gladly take it back, but they aren't going to refund your money. Who knows? You might need it when you receive a major award for your breakout novel," Max told her. Marty came in from the kitchen. "Thank God we are only providing appetizers and sandwiches for this thing. After all of this, I'm glad we're keeping it simple."

A hush came over the gathering as Evangeline entered in a red off-the-shoulder evening dress along with a ruby necklace that Nora was sure hadn't come from the secondhand store. She looked beautiful, and adoration shown in Doug's eyes. He was dressed in a dark navy suit and a gray silk tie. For it to be a night in Piney Woods, Texas, this little function felt like an after-party at the Oscars.

Nora picked up two of the wine glasses and handed them to Evangeline and Doug. "I'm so glad you stayed for the party."

They had expected Evangeline to check out and return to her home in New York, but Tuck's interview must have gone long.

Evangeline eyed Doug for a moment. "Doug convinced me to stay. I packed the dress just in case." She took a quick glance around the room and waved at the group of ladies gathered in the corner. "Glad I did now. My book sales are jumping. I think these ladies are going back to their rooms and ordering every book they can online," Evangeline whispered behind her hand.

"Besides the book sales, I'm glad she stayed a little longer, too. Very glad," Doug added with an admiring glance. Once again, Nora was touched by his devotion to Evangeline. That was something a lot of people seemed to have in buckets around her. "And where is your young man tonight?" Doug asked.

"He's still working. They are having a meeting tonight to discuss the two cases. Hopefully, he'll come by later. I can't believe we've had two murders in Piney Woods."

"Don't forget the catnapping," Doug smiled.

"That, too."

Izzy made her way into the informal grouping. "Good evening," she said, proffering a hand to Doug, who took it from her and, instead of kissing it, gave it a little shake.

Evangeline smiled, crinkling her nose slightly. "Izzy, how nice to see you again, and how lovely you look this evening. I thought you would be pounding away on that next draft."

"I am, but I just couldn't resist talking with you one more time. I hope you don't mind."

"Mind? I'm flattered. You are a very talented writer, and someday you'll realize you have the potential to go way beyond what I've done. I'll be getting writing advice from you."

Izzy glowed with pride. Evangeline had a way of saying just the right thing, and it showed on Izzy's face. Thanks to the mystery writer, she had enough go-juice to write ten novels now.

"I never really realized this before, but being around you and Izzy, I can see that writing is really a passion for you," Nora said. "It's much more than a job."

"Most days I would agree, but when I'm editing a manuscript for the umpteenth time, on that day it's definitely a job." There was laughter around Evangeline. She was the queen, holding court. She was not only the best-dressed attendee, but she was a bit taller than most of the women assembled. Nora knew this was her moment.

"You know," Nora said, "Alan Shaw certainly had that kind of passion for his writing. Did you know that he left a thumb drive in our business center computer with his writing on it? I guess writers today use things like this to store their work instead of all those stacks of paper. We don't really have a safe here, so I locked it in a drawer behind the front desk. I'm going to give it to his mother when she arrives tomorrow." Nora had no idea if Alan Shaw's mother was anywhere near the state of Texas, but judging from the interest of the group, her little story was ringing true.

Nora hoped Izzy would go along with her lie, even though she knew the truth. Izzy glanced at Nora and then added, "Virginia Woolf wrote in a pigsty. There is a lot of paperwork to be a writer. Keeping it on a thumb drive is a wonderful way to move your messy office from place to place."

"So right." Evangeline agreed. "It's such a pity about what happened to him. Tell me, Nora, did you look at what he was writing on the thumb drive? I've worked with many journalists, but I don't think I've ever met anyone, so..."

"Rude?" Izzy asked.

"I heard Camille say she was sorry that man ever set foot in our little convention. It certainly set a tone she didn't expect. Of course, now we know she wasn't always telling the truth. It makes me itch to write a catnapping in my next book," Evangeline added. With Martin-Ortega out of the picture, the convention goers would be paying their bills fair and square, and that was the end of it. Nora felt good about that.

"It was quite scandalous about what she did to Catpurnicus," Doug said. "It is unbelievable what some people will do for the evils of money."

"At least we got to meet all of you. We are all so pleased to have the Meow Meetup as guests, and we hope you enjoyed your stay here," Marty said.

"The Tunie is quite in demand," Nora said. "As soon as you check out, we are getting ready for a big party here tomorrow. I'm sure I'll be working late tonight after everyone else leaves."

"Oh, Nora, you don't have to do that," Marty said.

"I want to. I've been missing in action a lot lately, and it would be my pleasure to handle the clean-up here. I just hope I don't fall asleep, like I've seen Max do a few times."

Max gave a wink. "What can I say? That couch in the office can get pretty comfortable sometimes."

Nora had caught him asleep more than a few times. Luckily, the Tunie wouldn't have the kind of traffic they had right now with the Meow Meetup. She smiled at the assembled group. "I'll probably be home by midnight."

"You just have to be sure that you are. Your grandmother wouldn't want you out at all hours of the night. Why don't you let me stay with you?" Wiley said as he efficiently cleared a table.

"Honestly, everybody. I'll be fine. Uncle Wiley, I won't hear of you staying late. You've worked your tail off for this convention. I want you to go home and rest up."

Wiley shook his head. "If you say so."

Marty gave Nora a quizzical glance but then relented. "If you want to, the last thing I want to do is turn away a volunteer. I'm beat."

Max squeezed her shoulder. "We couldn't do this without you, Marty. Get your rest." Marty's eyes narrowed, suspicious of Nora's willingness to stay late.

"That's right," Nora broke in. "We need you. I'll take care of getting ready for Tatty and Ed's party tomorrow. Don't you worry about a thing?"

"Such devotion," Evangeline said as Doug nodded.

Chapter 35

As the party broke up and the members of the convention were exchanging addresses with promises to write, Doug strolled over to Nora, who was stacking chairs on tables for the vacuuming that was to follow. "Uh, Nora? I'd be careful tonight. You know, staying late and all. Will you be the only one here?"

"Yes. I told Dominic he didn't have to come in until midnight. He promised his ghost hunting group he would help set up some equipment at another haunted site, so that worked well for him."

"Yes. As you know, with Evangeline's visit to Piney Woods, I've really come to know her. I had no idea she had such a clamor of adoring fans. Some of these people are a little scary—case in point, Izzy. She is so determined about this book thing, and her temper frightens me a little. In this instance, she was there to protect her, which could be seen as noble, but you could also view her actions as a form of fanaticism."

Nora turned her head in surprise. Doug outweighed Izzy by seventy pounds. Surely, he couldn't be frightened of the little librarian. He took in Nora's expression. "I know it seems silly, but I'm just concerned for Evangeline. I don't know how equipped she really is to deal with a person like that. To be honest with you, when that woman went after Alan Shaw and then we found him dead, I guess I put two and two together. Maybe it's an assumption on my part."

Nora was touched by Doug's show of kindness toward the mystery writer. Maybe with whatever Alan Shaw had dug up about her past in the sixties, having someone like Doug around couldn't hurt.

"You're a good man, Doug Lindstrom."

He blushed at her compliment and then straightened his tie. "Thank you and good night."

After a polite handshake, Nora expected him to leave through the lobby, but instead he turned and stepped into the elevator. Old-fashioned politeness aside, it looked like Doug was spending the night in Evangeline's room, and Nora highly approved.

One by one, the kitchen staff departed. As Wiley pulled on a jacket and headed for the door, Nora called out to him. "Bye, Uncle Wiley. Good job tonight."

He simply nodded and headed out. Nora could see he was doing everything he had in his power to survive this battle he was waging with alcohol. Keeping his emotions in check seemed to be part of it, and for that reason, she let him walk out with barely a word. She just had to hope they would find their way back to each other. If he could go against his grain by reaching out to Corey, then maybe he would once again reach out to her. Nora was alone in the lobby. The lights in the banquet room and dining room were off, and she spent some time in the office finishing off bookwork generated by the convention guests and their array of payment options.

She kept the door open so she could keep an eye on the front desk. She had to hope she'd made enough noise at the party to alert whoever might be desperate enough to take the thumb drive. One thing she hadn't revealed was if the article Alan Shaw had been writing about Evangeline was indeed on the memory stick. The thumb drive had been substituted with another empty drive. After a little more research on the internet, Nora figured Alan Shaw had been tracking members of the Sunshine Brigade, who had all gone underground after a bombing that killed a man in Oakland, California. None of the members had surfaced in decades, and finding even one of them would have been quite the scoop. Pulitzer Prize material, for sure. Alan was sure he had found one of the members of the brigade in Evangeline, but with the name Francine Howard of Bridgeport, Connecticut. Looking at the picture Shaw had produced of Francine, Evangeline could be the same person, but age changes a person's face and body so much that it wasn't a solid identification. It was similar enough that if the police looked into it, Evangeline might have some explaining to do.

Francine had been running with a group of young people, numbering from ten to twenty participants. Even if she was a part of the group, they would have a hard time proving she was the one who set off the bomb and killed the poor janitor who lived in the basement.

Nora ran the sweeper through the lobby one more time as she cleaned after the day's festivities. Even though the conference attendees did not bring their cats, she could feel the cat dander everywhere. She had forgotten to take an allergy pill in all her rush to get ready, and she felt her eyes watering and her nose begin to run. After Nora finished her bookwork, she moved to the couch in the office, still watching the locked drawer. It was more comfortable than the office chair and almost impossible to see from the front desk. The quietness of the hotel reminded her of the first nights she ever worked there. She was sure then that the ghost of old Mr. Tunie, a dapper gentleman who wore a bow tie and loved to host dances in the banquet room, seemed to be with her during those quiet times. Right now, she felt alone and unsure of the trap she had tried to set. The thousands of steps, decisions, and endless efforts of her day started to set in, and she found herself agreeing with Max about the comfort of the couch growing with the hour. She started to drift off when she heard the rustle of feet in the lobby. The lighting was low, but there was a figure behind the front desk, working hard to open the locked drawer. Surprisingly, after less than a minute, the drawer opened. Nora jumped up and entered the lobby. If she could get a picture with her phone, then she would have the proof the police needed to nail Alan Shaw's killer. Just as she stepped quietly into the lobby and raised her phone, a powerful sneeze overtook her.

The person behind the counter jumped back, but then a tall form could be seen clearly from across the lobby.

"Doug?" Nora said this through a sniff. Doug Lindstrom stood holding the substitute flash drive. There was no mistaking that he was there for any other reason. He had to be the person who pushed Alan Shaw down the elevator shaft. Nora had suspected it was him, especially after she found a piece of white fluff by the elevator. It was nothing like the cat hair that was now being vacuumed up all over the hotel. It was coarse poodle hair. The same fur that Doug had pulled off his jacket the first night he dined at the Tunie with Evangeline.

"Nora. I was wondering if you had any..."

"Skip it. I was really hoping it wasn't you, but it just had to be."

"I don't know what you're talking about."

"I think you do. One of the things I admired about you was the devotion you showed to Evangeline. It was an example for the rest of us. You wouldn't let any harm come to her, so much so that when Alan Shaw threatened to expose her as a member of the Sunshine Brigade, you pushed him down the elevator shaft. That is how it happened, isn't it?"

"What are you talking about? Sunshine Brigade?" He answered innocently. So much so, Nora had to hope she was right.

"I can prove it, you know. I was quite impressed by your old-fashioned ways in that you never went above this floor when you visited Evangeline. She might have been a part of the free love of the 1960s, but you were always the gentleman. That's why, in the middle of a cat convention, I was shocked to find a small white piece of poodle hair under an end table by the elevator. That would have to mean that you had been up on that floor prior to tonight. You were up there the night Alan died, and I think you were the one who pushed him.

The only thing I can't figure out is why. It's one thing to protect your favorite writer, but you had to have a pretty strong reason to want to kill him."

Doug gulped. "You don't have anything on me. What if I was protective of Evangeline? There is no way you could ever understand."

"Try me."

"She was a part of something big. What the Sunshine Brigade did was in the name of peace. Nobody was supposed to die. We didn't know there was an old man in the basement. Killing was against our principles."

Nora bit her bottom lip. "Are you saying that you, too, were part of the Sunshine Brigade?"

He stopped suddenly. Nora realized he thought she already knew this fact about him. She pushed on. "You were a part of the same protest group? You've been underground here in Piney Woods all these years? What was your name back then? I already know Evangeline used to be Francine Howard, and if I don't know who you are now, it shouldn't take long for me to figure out who you were."

"What the hell?" Doug Lindstrom's kindly face took on a hard edge. "My real name is Duncan. Duncan Leach. Of the Boston Leach's, as if that mattered to anyone anymore. I came from a family that had houses in Boston, New Rochelle, and an apartment in New York. Establishment: upper-class snobs who had no idea what the real world was like. They didn't know about the pain and killing the war was causing. People were out there suffering man, but they didn't care, especially if it interfered with cocktail hour. I had to tell my story, that's all."

"And it killed three men. One in the sixties and two right here."

"Like I said, you don't understand. If that article had been published, then Evangeline would have been outed, and it wouldn't take the police long to figure out where I was. Duncan Leach is wanted for murder. Doug Lindstrom is not. I couldn't have either of those two bottom-feeder reporters find out. It had to be done."

Why was he telling her so much information about his past crimes? Was he planning on killing her the way he ended the life of Alan Shaw? According to Janice Joplin, freedom was just another word for nothing else to lose. He was looking at the possibility of losing his. Somehow, when she planned this giant "catch the killer" trap, she didn't account for the fact that the killer might not come along willingly. A possible fatal error on her part. She had to think and think fast.

"You know, I've been recording this whole conversation."

She eyed the lobby door. She was closer to it than he was. She could run out of the hotel and straight into the police station.

"Have you?" He pocketed the thumb drive. "What a waste of data! Good luck trying to get video from a smashed phone. That's right! You're dating the police fellow. What's his name? Huck?"

"Tuck," said a voice from the darkness. Was somebody else here? Has somebody else been listening to this whole conversation? Nora was somewhere between scrambling for her own self-preservation and relief. He could smash her phone, but killing two people was a pretty tall order.

Wiley stepped out of the darkness. "I loved the sixties, man, but I sure as hell didn't blow anything up like you did. What you're saying to Nora is right. We don't understand, but I never have understood people who are crazy enough to justify murder."

Doug twitched as he looked from Wiley to Nora. "What do I need to do to make you forget all of this? Do you want money? I have a little saved up."

"We don't want your money," Nora said. "This isn't the kind of thing you can negotiate out of. What about Evangeline? Is she involved in this too?"

"No. Evangeline's innocent. Evangeline was always innocent. She didn't want to have anything to do with the Sunshine Brigade, but I pulled her into it. She wasn't around the night that the building blew up. Don't drag her into this. It's all me." Doug Lindstrom then reached in his pocket one more time. Nora was sure he would turn over the flash drive and give himself up at this point. Instead, he pulled a gun from his pocket and pointed it directly at Nora.

Wiley put both hands up. "Now you don't need to haul off and shoot anybody. We could maybe take a check or something."

"Drop the gun!" Tuck shouted from the doorway.

"You know," Wiley said with a giggle, "you were worried about Nora's phone data, but I have to admit I used mine all up texting ol' Tucker here about your big confession. I'm not sure if I spelled brigade right, though. I was never too good in school. I have been told I can fry the hell out of a chicken."

"Drop the gun!" Tuck repeated.

Doug Lindstrom leveled his gun on Tuck, intending to shoot, but before he could pull the trigger, Tuck's bullet buzzed through the air, hitting Doug squarely in the chest. His cause, his love, and his protests were over.

Chapter 36

"Oh, Nora, you did such a beautiful job for our anniversary party," Tatty said as she rested her tired feet on a chair. "Even with everything that happened, this was the finest party we've ever had. Thank you so much."

"Glad to do it." Nora blushed.

Marty put an arm around her. "This lady right here is amazing. She brought us our first convention."

Max butted in, "And our first murder." As Max spoke, Nora couldn't help but notice that he was holding Marty's hand. Had something happened between them? From the sparkle in Max's eyes, she had to assume that it had.

Marty bit her bottom lip and then let out a contagious smile. That little action confirmed to Nora that two old friends were on their way to becoming more. Marty continued, "That too, but then she managed this wonderful anniversary party right after. I don't know if I said this before, but I don't know what I'd do without you."

Val came in, drying her hands on a dish towel, with Wiley following her. "I thought I'd give Wiley a hand in there. Being the newbie here, I feel like I have to prove myself. Nora's shadow can be pretty overwhelming sometimes."

Val's praise served as a balm to Nora's soul after feeling so threatened by her. Somehow now, her fear of inadequacy had left her.

If anything, she was happy to have Val on staff. Val had even offered to train Nora on any areas of management she was lacking.

"Speaking of that," the Frederick's sisters came over each with hands flapping their love beads as they walked. Azalea and Violet Fredericks had been regular visitors to the Tunie Hotel for their entire lives. They were also principle purveyors of gossip in the city of Piney Woods, Texas. "We heard you single-handedly apprehended that, dear Mr. Lindstrom. Weren't you frightened?"

"I heard you wrestled him to the ground," Azalea said.

"No, no. I heard she hit them over the head with a vase," Violet interrupted.

"I'm afraid you're both wrong. I may have proved that Doug Lindstrom was the murderer, but the apprehending of the suspect was done by Uncle Wiley and Tuck. I don't know what I would've done if they hadn't shown up."

Tuck came back to the table carrying two plates with psychedelic anniversary cake and placed one in front of Nora. "I don't know what you would've done either. One thing I've learned about this woman here is that she isn't afraid to let someone know what she thinks. Doug Lindstrom was no different. She told him she knew he was the murderer."

"And then Uncle Wiley showed up."

"I never left, darlin'," he said as he pulled out a chair, sitting down in exhaustion. "You were just too blatant about volunteering to be all alone in the hotel late at night. Tuck is right. You are transparent. Even then, I didn't do any good."

"Yes, you did. You texted Tuck, even though he was already here, but that is how I got out of that situation alive."

"With a big ol' gun."

"Oh my, I'm getting the vapors," Miss Azalea said, raising her hand to her forehead and causing her beads to clank.

"I have to know: what's going to happen to Evangeline?" Nora asked.

Tatty sat up, explaining what she knew about the investigation. "She's being investigated, but it seems she really had nothing to do with the bombing that killed the man. When I met her at Woodstock, it was Doug who she had been fighting with that day. They were broken up by then, but she was still tied to the organization."

"Yes, and from what I hear, Izzy has promised to sit in the courtroom every day behind Evangeline," Tuck said.

"That was what Evangeline did best. She gathered loyal admirers. First Doug, then Izzy," Nora said.

Tuck agreed with her. "Yeah, but even though Izzy might inflict some bodily harm, I doubt she would kill for her favorite writer. And really, Doug killed Alan Shaw because his snooping around would lead to him. Living underground for that many years had to make those times seem like a dream to the two of them. They had moved on with their lives, and meeting here, like this, was as if it had never happened. Still, when the Meow Meetup was choosing a location, Evangeline told them she wanted to come here."

"To be near Doug, I'll bet," Tatty said.

"You know how hard it is to resist the temptation of a handsome man," Ed said as he reached out and took Tatty's hand.

"Oh, yes, and if I ever forget, I'm sure you'll remind me." Tatty came back.

Ed brought her hand up to his mouth. "Mi Amore."

To her surprise, Corey Brockwell entered the banquet room and went over to shake Ed's hand. "Sorry, I'm a little late. Congratulations to you two. Seeing as you have single-handedly taken on my big sister, I thought you deserved acknowledgment. She can be a handful." He then turned to Nora.

"I think you'll find the Brockwell Industries statements fully up-to-date and in your mailbox tomorrow. My friend Wiley here stressed to me the importance of meeting my commitments. He's been a real inspiration."

Nora looked over to Wiley, who was sporting a wide grin. "That's the way to do it, son. Mend those fences. I know I have a few to mend."

After that, Corey talked a little longer and then politely excused himself. Nora would believe the statements were in the mail when she found the letter in her mailbox and not a minute sooner. Still, though, she appreciated his effort. Maybe with Wiley's help, there was hope for him yet. Today was going a little better than the day before between the two of them. Time was starting to heal the argument that had occurred between them. "Let me help with the table clearing," Nora said.

"You don't have to," Wiley said, rising from his chair.

"I know," she said softly. "I want to." As the two of them started loading plates into the dirty dish cart, Nora spoke to her uncle. "I'm sorry about what I said. I didn't know Corey was your sponsor. I should have trusted you. It's just that the two of you have nothing in common. Nothing."

"I should have told you. When you spend your whole life sneaking drinks, you forget how important it is to let other people know what you're doing. If it's any comfort to you, I'm still sober. I've stayed that way, but not without the group and now Corey. He's staying sober and away from gambling, too. He still has a lot of his old man in him, poor kid, and that will just have to iron out with time, but he's trying. We're both trying, and yes, we both have something in common. You. I'm trying to do well because I love you, and I'm getting to know the niece who came to me so late in life. Corey is trying to do better because he doesn't want you breathing down his back about those Brockwell Industry earnings. Either way, it's all about you, Nora."

Nora kissed Wiley on the cheek and hugged him. "Thank you."

"For what? Not being a screw-up? Now I'm serious. I think you need to spend some time with your fella." He gazed over at Tuck, who grinned.

"Now that's what I like to see," Rosalyn said as she came upon them in her walker. Lucy and Arnette walked on either side of Nora's grandmother. "My son and my granddaughter are getting along. Your mama would be so proud."

"I hope so."

"Your mama was always proud of you. From the moment you were born, when you went through that awkward stage and wanted a tattoo, to the first kiss you had on that class trip. I don't know if you ever knew that."

Nora felt a surge of something she hadn't been feeling the last few days, and she couldn't quite put her finger on it. Was this acceptance? Confidence? Self Esteem? It was amazing how just a few little words can make a world of difference. She looked over to Tuck, who was now gathering dishes into stacks. He caught her glance and gave a low, smoldering smile that made the back of Nora's neck heat up. Not only were things better with Wiley, it seemed.

"I'm glad to know that, Grandma Rosalyn."

"Stow that in your heart, baby girl. The love you find will always be there. I didn't get to have your mama here for so many years, but I always put a little piece of memory deep in my heart and pulled it out on those days I missed her the most."

Nora hugged her grandmother, and then Lucy's phone made a beeping sound. "Hate to rush you ladies, but I have a date."

Nora pulled away. "A date? You just got back into town. Who could you be dating?"

"My little secret." Lucy said. Since she and her mother had returned from New York, Lucy had barely been around. What was she doing that was taking up all her time? Had she brought back some sexy Manhattan mogul?

"Uh huh." Arnette said, rolling her eyes.

Once Nora's family left, she went to retrieve her purse, thinking about all her grandmother had said to her. It was like a warm blanket going around her shoulders, thinking about her mother's love, and then she stopped. If her mother hadn't been around Rosalyn all those years, how could she have known about the kiss? Or the tattoo?

"About ready?" Tuck said, coming up behind her and slipping his hands around her waist.

"Wait." Nora said, pulling away. "I would just like to say thank you."

"For what?"

"For hiding in my lobby and saving..."

"Your precious behind," Tuck smiled. "My pleasure. I know we both had some stuff going on, but no matter who comes sauntering into your lobby, I'd like you to know that I'm happy with you. That and I've come to really like that behind."

Nora looked lovingly around the Tunie Hotel, her hotel.

"It'll be quiet around here tonight, thank goodness." Nora felt the weariness of the last week flooding through her. Tuck nibbled on her ear. "Maybe, maybe not."

Nora laughed as Tuck's kiss tickled her neck. It was a feeling she wanted to have for years to come.

Don't miss out!

Visit the website below and you can sign up to receive emails whenever Teresa Trent publishes a new book. There's no charge and no obligation.

https://books2read.com/r/B-A-FJQD-PMBDD

BOOKS 2 READ

Connecting independent readers to independent writers.

Did you love *A Sneeze to Die For*? Then you should read *Murder of a Good Man*[1] by Teresa Trent!

[2]

When Nora Alexander drives into Piney Woods, Texas, to fulfill her dying mother's last wish, she has no idea what awaits her. First she is run off the road, then the sealed letter she delivers turns out to be a scathing rebuke to the town's most beloved citizen and favored candidate for Piney Woods Pioneer: Adam Brockwell. Next thing you know, Adam has been murdered in a nasty knife attack. Suspicion instantly falls on Nora, one of the last people to see him alive. After all, everyone in Piney Woods loved him. Or did they? Turns out Nora's mother had a complicated past she never shared with her daughter.

Told not to leave town by Tuck the flirty sheriff, Nora finds a job with Tuck's Aunt Marty trying to get the rundown Tunie Hotel back

1. https://books2read.com/u/meq2vz

2. https://books2read.com/u/meq2vz

in the black. The old hotel was Piney Woods' heart and soul in its heyday as an oil boomtown. Now the secrets it harbors may be the key to getting Nora off the hook. She's going to need to solve the mystery quickly to avoid arrest, or worse: becoming the killer's next victim.

Book 1 in the Piney Woods Mystery series.

Read more at https://teresatrent.com.

Also by Teresa Trent

Pecan Bayou
A Dash of Murder
Overdue for Murder
Doggone Dead
Buzzkill
Burnout
Murder for a Rainy Day
Till Dirt Do Us Part
Oh Holy Fright
Die a Yellow Ribbon

Piney Woods
Murder of a Good Man
A Sneeze to Die For
Die Die Blackbird

Redbird Creek
The Con Man's Daughter

Watch for more at https://teresatrent.com.